CASSIE EDWARDS, AUTHOR OF THE *SAVAGE* SERIES

Winner of the *Romantic Times* Lifetime Achievement Award for Best Indian Series!

HESITANT CAPTOR

"I do not ask for the white woman," Gray Eyes said. "My friend will you take her?"

Blue Thunder hesitated. He had never wanted captives of any sort, especially those with white skin. He had no wish to give the white pony soldiers cause to come to his village because a white woman was there.

But…this was not just any white woman. He had seen enough of her to know that she was someone who intrigued him to the very core of his being. He slowly nodded as he took slow steps toward Shirleen, his gaze never leaving her green eyes. "Yes, I will take her."

Shirleen trembled as Blue Thunder stepped up to her, his eyes reaching into her soul it seemed.

CASSIE EDWARDS

SAVAGE SKIES

LEISURE BOOKS   NEW YORK CITY

A LEISURE BOOK®

September 2007

Published by

Dorchester Publishing Co., Inc.
200 Madison Avenue
New York, NY 10016

ISBN-10: 0-8439-5537-6
ISBN-13: 978-0-8439-5537-8

The name "Leisure Books" and the stylized "L" with design are
trademarks of Dorchester Publishing Co., Inc.

Printed in the United States of America.

Visit us on the web at www.dorchesterpub.com.

I lovingly dedicate Savage Skies, *my 100th published book, to my husband Charlie. It was Charlie who believed in me and in my ability to write the first book before I believed in myself. Thank you, sweet Charlie!*

Also, in friendship, and a big thank you, I dedicate Savage Skies *to a dear friend, Nancy McGennis, who many years ago loaned me one of her books to read....an historical romance. It was the very first historical romance that I ever read and I immediately became hooked on that genre of books, so much that I decided to write one myself. That first book was published as well as all the others that I have written since then. Thank you, Nancy, for giving me the inspiration to write. I can't imagine what my life would be had I never known the love of writing!*

With much appreciation I dedicate my 100th book to Alicia Condon, my very special editor at Dorchester, who has played a major role in my success as an author. Thank you, Alicia!

I also thank John Prebich, president and publisher of Dorchester Publishing, as well as the entire Dorchester staff, for helping make my Savage Series *the success that it has become!*

And now, on to my next 100!

Love,
Cassie

He rode quickly and stealthily through the night,
Heart racing, never stopping until he had her in sight.
Long, waist-length auburn hair,
Blowing in the night breeze without care.
Eyes that penetrate and shine like the bright sky,
To see her again he had to tell a forbidden lie.
How could he be so dishonest, their noble chief,
At that thought his heart ached with such grief.
Oh, Great Spirit, from up above,
Please help my people accept the woman I deeply love.

—Melissa Duncan,
Poet, fan, and friend

SAVAGE SKIES

Chapter One

Through many changing years
We have shared each other's gladness,
And we wept each other's tears. . . .

—Jefferys

Wyoming, 1851
Autumn—the moon when the calf grows hair

The sun spiraled lazily down the smoke hole of the largest tepee in the village of the Wind Band of Assiniboine Indians, a name which meant literally "our people."

This was the lodge of Chief Wa-ke-un-to, Blue Thunder. Twenty-eight winters of age, he was a muscled and boldly handsome man. His sculpted features contrasted vividly with the pockmarked face of the man who sat with him in private council.

Gray Eyes was a dear childhood friend of Blue Thunder and chief of the neighboring White Owl Band of Assiniboine.

"It is good to have you sitting with me again, my friend," Blue Thunder said. "Tell me why you have need of council with your friend Blue Thunder. I am always here to listen and to offer help, if it is needed."

"I come with sad news," Gray Eyes said

solemnly. "I hate to ask for your help again, my friend, but times are hard for my people, and this time our misfortune is not of my doing. I need to ask your warriors' assistance in a task that will be dangerous for us all."

The tail feather of an eagle hung from a lock of hair at the right side of Gray Eyes' head as the mark of his chieftaincy.

He gazed at his friend, who wore a similar feather in his own long, black hair. Like Gray Eyes, Blue Thunder was attired in fringed buckskin and moccasins.

"Never feel ashamed of the trouble life has brought you, but take from it the strength to make things better again for your people," Blue Thunder said, gazing at his friend's pock-marked face.

It was so disfigured, Blue Thunder could barely recognize him. Blue Thunder had warned his friend not to go to the white man's trading post while the disease called smallpox was killing so many white and red-skinned people.

Knowing of the danger, Blue Thunder had separated his own band from others during this time. As a result, the Wind Band remained unscathed by the disease.

For a moment Blue Thunder wondered if he should risk the lives of his warriors to help a chief who had disregarded Blue Thunder's earlier warnings.

Should he tell Gray Eyes that he must live with the decision that now haunted him?

But no, Blue Thunder loved Gray Eyes as

much as he would love a brother. The two had learned to shoot and ride together as children, and he knew that he could not refuse his friend anything.

"Tell me now about the problem that has brought you here today," Blue Thunder invited.

He slid a wooden tray of various foods, both meats and fruits, closer to his friend, who still refused to choose anything.

It was apparent that food was the farthest thing from Gray Eyes' mind, and Blue Thunder was anxious to know what caused such distress.

"I have come to sit with you and talk alone with you, having left my remaining warriors to protect the survivors of a recent ambush on my village by the Comanche renegade, Big Nose," Gray Eyes said, his voice drawn with emotion. "The Comanche knew how weakened my people were from smallpox. Our band has been reduced from one hundred fifty lodges to eighty. Big Nose took advantage of this weakness and captured not only many of my strongest warriors, but also a great number of our horses."

"And you want vengeance," Blue Thunder guessed. He chose a piece of venison from the tray and took a bite, his eyes gazing intently into Gray Eyes'.

"I want more than that," Gray Eyes said, his gaze suddenly aflame with hate. And then his look softened into concern. "I want my warriors back, or my band will not survive. Will you ride with me, Blue Thunder, to go and re-claim what is mine? Will you choose your best warriors to accompany us? Getting back what is mine will not be easy. Some may die to res-cue my warriors. Are you prepared to chance that? Or would you rather I leave and set out after Big Nose with the few warriors who are left to ride with me?"

Gray Eyes lowered his gaze. "I am asking too much of my friend this time," he said thickly.

He ran a hand across his pock-scarred brow. Feeling the scars was always a reminder of what he had so unwisely done.

He had taken his warriors to that trading post, even though he'd heard the rumors that it was overrun by the white man's disease.

But the pelts that he had for trade that year had been too good not to take the chance. He and his men had been eager to get what they could from the richest pelts they'd hunted in many a moon.

And there were only four or five months out of a full year when the fur of the animals was marketable. The rest of the year, his warriors killed only enough to provide meat, clothing, and lodges for their families.

If he had not taken advantage of that special time when he'd had so many plush pelts, he knew that someone else would have filled the shelves of the trading post, leaving no space for his furs.

So he had chanced everything, and had lost in the worst way.

Ho, yes, he had gotten what was due him in trade, but the sacrifice had been the most terrible any village of people could suffer.

Many had died, and those who had not were scarred for life.

"Please do not lower your eyes in shame," Blue Thunder said. He reached over and placed a comforting hand on his friend's shoulder. "My friend, you know that I would never let you down, even if you did refuse to listen to my warning about the white man's disease. You have already paid the price of not heeding my warning, and now it is time to forget and to move forward."

Gray Eyes lifted his chin and gazed directly into Blue Thunder's eyes. "You will join me then to hunt for the Comanche who came and killed and stole from Gray Eyes and his people?" he asked hopefully. "I fear that if you do not help me, my small band is doomed. We will eventually lose everything."

"I am very aware of all of this," Blue Thunder said, slowly nodding his head. He moved his hand from Gray Eyes' shoulder. "Now is the time to look forward, not backward."

"I should have listened to you about the smallpox," Gray Eyes said tightly. "I never should have gone to that trading post, but the hunt seemed too good to ignore. I had the best pelts I'd seen in many moons. So did all of my warriors. Their pride matched mine. We were blinded by that pride, my friend. Now many of those valiant warriors are no longer with us."

"You must leave behind such regret and look forward to the future," Blue Thunder encouraged. He gazed intently into his friend's eyes. "Where there is hope, there is a way. I will do everything I can to help you build on that hope."

"Blue Thunder, my best friend in the world, instead of bringing my people great riches, I brought them the greatest misfortune," Gray Eyes said thickly. "Even more devastating than war! My people have gained nothing by intimacy with whites but disease and heartbreak."

"Smallpox has destroyed the lives of many people with red skin," Blue Thunder said, slowly nodding. "Like you, too many of our people chose to ignore the dangers of associating with whites. The price paid has been hard to bear."

"I am grateful I had a friend such as you to help in our time of trouble," Gray Eyes said. He placed a hand on Blue Thunder's muscled shoulder. "You have always been a true friend. How can I ever repay you for such friendship?"

"No payment, or thanks, is needed," Blue Thunder said as Gray Eyes slowly lowered his hand from his shoulder. "*Hakamya-upo*, come. Come with me now. I will go outside and announce a quick council. We will meet and discuss how we can get the best of the renegades. Big Nose has been a thorn in my side for too long. Some even say he was the one responsible for the death of my wife. It is time for him to be stopped."

"*Ho*, it is time to rescue my warriors," Gray Eyes said, stepping from the tepee with Blue Thunder. "I have prayed to *Wah-con-tun-ga*, the Greatness who looks down over us all, that he will help make the wrongs suffered right."

"After our council we will leave to track down Big Nose and those who follow him. We will bring home the warriors taken by them," Blue Thunder said, walking alongside Gray Eyes to the center of the village. There, Blue Thunder would make his announcement about the council and why it was being held.

He turned to Gray Eyes. "We will also retrieve your horses," he promised.

"*Pila-maye*," Gray Eyes said, humbly thanking Blue Thunder.

Chapter Two

I believe love, pure and true,
Is to the soul a sweet,
Immortal dew.

—Townsend

A cool breeze wafted through the bedroom window, fluttering the sheer curtains over the bed as Shirleen Mingus folded clothes, then slid them into her embroidered travel bag.

A keen sadness swept through her at the thought of what life was forcing upon her. After traveling from Boston with her husband and three other families to settle in Wyoming, Shirleen was now planning another journey. She wished she were back where she had been the happiest.

And that had been before she had met and wed her husband, Earl.

While courting Shirleen, he had been a consummate actor, for he was nothing like the man he'd appeared to be when she had accepted his hand in marriage.

Even her parents had been fooled.

Although they had not wanted their

seventeen-year-old daughter to move so far away, fearing they would never see her again, they had felt satisfied that she would have a good husband who would treat her with love and respect.

She would never forget those last moments with her papa. He had run his fingers slowly through her long, red hair as he peered through tears into her green eyes, saying that he feared the long journey out west would be hard on her because she was so petite. He had called her his tiny, pretty thing, so slender that he could place his hands around her waist, his fingertips meeting behind her.

But when she had reassured him that the man she was marrying loved her with all of his heart and had vowed to protect her, and that she had no doubt he was capable of both things, her father had given his final blessing.

Now she was twenty-one and had learned the hard way just how wrong she had been about the man she'd married. He had been abusive to her ever since they'd arrived in Wyoming, taking the belt to her at every opportunity. He beat her when he found the slightest fault in anything she did around the house, or with their daughter Megan. He believed she would never leave him because her parents were too far away for her to flee back to their protective, loving arms.

But Earl was wrong. At this very moment, while Earl was on his way to the trading post with his two neighbor friends, Shirleen was taking advantage of this opportunity to flee from someone she considered a madman.

She was going to escape this life she abhorred.

She was not sure where she would go, for she did not have the money to travel back to Boston. But no matter what, she must flee this man who she feared might one day kill her.

The dear Lord above would guide her to a better, safer place.

Her Bible, her prayers, and her daughter were all that had kept her going these past months when Earl had beaten her daily, all the while using foul curse words that their daughter Megan overheard.

Now and then, the sweet child used one of those words herself because she had no idea that it was wrong to speak them. Her papa had said those words. That made it alright in her young mind.

A tugging at the skirt of Shirleen's dress brought her out of her deep thoughts.

She turned and gazed down at her four-year-old daughter Megan. The child's blue eyes and golden hair had been inherited from her father, while her tininess had come from her mother.

Shirleen had been married at the age of seventeen and had become with child soon after, while on the grueling trip to Wyoming.

A small grave had been left beside the road on the day Shirleen's abused body aborted that first child.

While their traveling companions were fetching water from a creek, Earl had taken exception to her soft complaint about the heat. He doubled his right hand into a tight fist and hit Shirleen so hard that she had fallen from the wagon, landing on her stomach.

Within the hour she had aborted the child and had learned what the word *hate* meant, although she had been taught that hatred was sinful.

But she had hated Earl from the first time he'd hit her right up until this morning when he had given her the usual punch before setting out for the trading post.

Their friends had never learned what sort of man Earl was, for he had put on a good show, appearing to be the most thoughtful of husbands while they were around. But he treated Shirleen like a punching bag when they were alone, when he was not lashing her with his horrible belt.

"Mama, can I go and play with the baby chicks? Can I?" Megan asked, her blue eyes wide as she gazed up at Shirleen.

Seeing the innocence of her child, Shirleen swept her daughter into her arms. Megan was one of the reasons Shirleen knew she must leave. Earl had never beaten the little girl, but Shirleen had no doubt that he would once Megan was older. She and her daughter must be far away from him before that happened.

"Oh, how I love you," Shirleen murmured as she gave Megan a soft hug. "You are all that I have in this world, and I must protect you, darlin'. We are going to leave soon, Megan. We are going on an adventure together. We are going on that adventure today."

"Papa not go?" Megan asked, stroking her tiny fingers through her mother's long, red hair.

"Papa not go," Shirleen said, nodding. "But that is alright. We will have fun without him."

"Can we take the baby chicks with us?" Megan asked, searching her mother's eyes.

"No, I don't think so," Shirleen murmured. She fought back the tears that came so easily these past days at the thought of what she must do, and the dangers of doing it.

They lived in a wild land, where renegade Indians roamed and killed every day.

But that was the chance she must take in order to survive. She was sure that one day Earl's meanness would end in her death.

What then would become of her precious daughter?

The thought of Megan living alone with such a man as Earl turned her insides cold. He was capable of all sorts of cruelty.

"But I love the chicks, Mama," Megan whined. "Don't you?"

"Yes, but I love you more, and you are all that I want to take with me on our exciting journey," Shirleen said, still trying to make the trip ahead sound like fun to her child.

"Can I go now and play with the chicks?" Megan asked, squirming out of Shirleen's arms.

Shirleen pushed herself up to a standing position, placed a hand at the small of her back, which ached from her morning beating, and nodded. "Yes, you can go now and see the baby chicks, but be careful when you pet them," she said softly. "Like you, they are tiny and fragile."

Shirleen walked Megan from the bedroom to the front door of their four-room log cabin.

"Wait, Megan," she said. "It's cool this morning. You'd better wear a wrap."

She reached for a sweater she had recently finished knitting for Megan. As Megan had watched, Shirleen had embroidered tiny baby chicks on the upper left side of the sweater.

She knelt down and placed the sweater on her daughter, securing the top button, then stood and watched Megan run from the house, squealing with delight at the prospect of holding one of the tiny chicks again.

Not trusting anything her husband did these days, Shirleen peered from the door to check that the front gate was closed so that her daughter could go no farther than the yard.

She sighed with relief when she saw that Earl had latched the gate.

Now Shirleen must hurry to finish packing. The time had finally arrived. She was actually going to flee this marriage she so despised.

These past two days, it had been difficult to find moments to prepare for her departure without Earl becoming aware of it before he left for the trading post.

But she had managed to prepare a bag of provisions, which included food, clothing, blankets, and other necessities. She had hidden them beneath her bed, ready for the moment when she would leave.

She knew that she must travel by the fastest means possible in order to get as far as she could before her husband found her missing. Consequently, she had chosen to make her escape on horseback. Using a buggy would slow her down too much.

She had made a little sack from leather to put her daughter in, which would hang from the side of the horse, while on the other side she would fasten their sack of provisions.

Breathless now that the moment was finally at hand, Shirleen hurried to the bedroom and fell to her knees beside the bed. Her hand trembled as she reached beneath the bed and pulled the rest of her belongings from beneath it.

Her heart pounding, she secured a shawl around her shoulders, a bonnet on her head, then gazed at a rifle that she knew she must take with her. Who was to say who or what might become a threat?

Although she did not know how to fire a rifle, she knew that just having a gun would provide some protection. Most men would leave her alone if she was pointing a rifle at them.

As for wild animals, she'd just have to pray that she could shoot the rifle well enough to scare them away with the report of the firearm.

She grabbed it, then stepped out on the porch with Megan's travel bag and her own, and the sack of provisions.

She sucked in a deep breath and felt the color drain from her face when she saw that the front gate was no longer closed, but gaping open. She also saw that the baby chicks were running free all over the yard.

Worst of all, Megan was nowhere in sight!

Panic filled her, and she dropped her bags and the rifle and ran from the porch, crying Megan's name.

Then she almost fainted from fear when more than one flaming arrow flew past her, slamming into the barn, which soon caught fire.

"Megan!" she screamed as she ran in the direction of the open gate. Sudden whoops and hollers filled the air, while the sound of horses' hoofbeats rumbled like the thunder of a horrendous summer storm.

Tears rolled from Shirleen's eyes at the realization that Megan was gone. Oh, Lord, surely she was dead, and Shirleen was living her own last moments of life.

Suddenly she stopped, frozen stiff, when the Indians, their faces painted with black and red war paint, rode out of the shadows of a great stretch of trees just beyond her fence.

She watched, wild-eyed, as their horses leaped over the fence and thundered toward her.

The last thing she knew was paralyzing fear for Megan. Then a club hit her across the back of her head, rendering her unconscious.

Behind her, and on past her yard, fires raged as the nearby homes and barns were set afire by the flaming arrows, while people Shirleen had grown to love as much as brothers and sisters fell, one by one, at the hands of the murdering, heartless renegades.

And then there was silence.

Chapter Three

More firm and sure the hand
Of courage strikes,
When it obeys the watchful
Eye of caution.

—Thomson

Blue Thunder and Gray Eyes and Blue Thunder's warriors rode across the land. They were searching for any signs of the Comanche renegades led by the fierce and fearless Big Nose. These renegades were giving the Comanche people a bad name, leaving a swath of bloodshed behind them wherever they rode. But Blue Thunder had a more personal reason for wanting to hunt them down. He had reason to believe that they might be the ones responsible for the brutal rape and killing of his lovely young wife, Shawnta.

After Blue Thunder had lost sight of the tracks he had been following, he wasn't certain where to look for Big Nose. The renegade was known to change his hideout often in order to keep anyone from finding it.

Blue Thunder and Gray Eyes had agreed that they would ride until dark today, and if

they didn't find Big Nose, they would resume
the search tomorrow.

They were determined not to give up. Blue
Thunder would not rest until he knew whether
Big Nose was the one who'd killed his wife, and
Gray Eyes had vowed to rescue his warriors.

Suddenly Blue Thunder drew rein and
stopped his steed, followed by the others.
Ahead, all could see the huge billows of black
smoke not far away.

"There are no villages near here, so what is
burning must be a white settlement," Blue
Thunder said. "*Hakamya-upo*, come. Let us go
and see if there are any survivors."

They rode hard toward the smoke.

Soon they discovered three cabins aflame,
where settlers had lived in close proximity to
each other.

They rode onward and stopped close to one
of the raging fires. The sight that met their
eyes made Blue Thunder's stomach churn
with disgust.

He swallowed hard and looked away from
the dead bodies. Those who had came today
and ambushed these white people had not
stopped at killing the women, but also their
children, who lay scattered on the ground.

And all had been scalped.

Blue Thunder did not have to take a closer
look at the women to know that they had been
raped, for their skirts were hiked up past their
waists, leaving their lower bodies exposed.

"There are no men," Gray Eyes said as he sidled his horse closer to Blue Thunder's. "The coward renegades took full advantage of the innocent while their men were away."

"The men, even the sons, are more than likely at the trading post, unaware of what they will find when they return," Blue Thunder said, his voice full of loathing for whoever had done this.

He had to admit that he was not a lover of white people, but he did not hate them enough to kill and ravage their women.

He had learned to keep his distance from white people, except for those he dealt with at the trading post at Fort Dennison.

He would only attack whites if they attacked him first.

If at all possible, he avoided war.

"This is the work of Big Nose," Blue Thunder announced. He shook his head. "And it seems he has gotten careless this time. The cabins and barns are still burning, so he cannot be far from here."

"*Ho*, that is so," Gray Eyes said, smiling smugly. "Let us follow the tracks. We shall surely find him soon."

Blue Thunder dismounted.

He studied the various tracks, and then followed some to a fence that had been ripped out of the ground. From there, many tracks of both horses and people on foot came together.

He looked quickly over at Gray Eyes. "He has taken captives," he said, frowning. "Perhaps *that* is why we saw no white men. They have all surely been taken captive."

"The horses from all three homesteads are missing," said Proud Horse, one of Blue Thunder's most loyal warriors, as he ran up to him.

"And so they not only took captives as their spoils of war, but also *mitasunkes*, horses." Blue Thunder nodded. "I would have thought they would only want *mitasunkes*. Taking captives is unwise, for it will not only awaken more hatred against the red man, but it will also slow Big Nose down."

Gray Eyes bent to a knee and studied the footprints. "*Ho*, the white captives are made to walk, not ride," he reported. "That will slow the renegades."

"He has made one mistake after another today," Blue Thunder said. He slowly kneaded his chin. "I wonder if it is on purpose. Or has he finally made an unwise decision?"

"Why would he do this on purpose?" Gray Eyes asked, slowly standing.

"He might want to lure those who will follow into a trap so that he can have more captives," Blue Thunder suggested. "I think it is time that his plans are foiled, no matter what they may be."

Blue Thunder turned and gazed again at the death and destruction all around him. He swallowed hard as his gaze fell upon the dead women.

He went to the first one and then another and lowered the skirts of their dresses over their nakedness, trying to give them some dignity in death.

He then ran to his horse and leaped onto its back. "Let us ride!" he shouted, a fist in the air.

He lowered his fist and gave Gray Eyes a slow smile. "Today we will not only find the white survivors, but also the warriors who were taken from your village," he said.

Gray Eyes nodded, his eyes filled with flame; then they rode off, side by side, with Blue Thunder's warriors following behind them.

As they rode off, the smoke still spiraled into the sky, and Blue Thunder looked over his shoulder at the devastation left behind by a demon who had no heart, and surely no soul.

"Big Nose, I know you did this. I will find you and you will pay for your heartless ways, not only toward whites, but to all," he whispered to himself.

He looked straight ahead, the renegades' tracks leading him onward. The sun was now making lengthy shadows of the trees, and the cool breeze of late afternoon had sprung up.

His jaw was set tight in his determination to find Big Nose. The other times he had searched for him, his efforts had been in vain.

But today?

Ho, today, he felt confident that Big Nose had become careless, careless enough to finally be stopped!

Chapter Four

All's to be fear'd,
Where all is to be lost.

—Byron

The sun beat down on Shirleen, almost blinding her as she walked wearily along with the other captives. They were all roped together in a long line, being led by renegades on horseback.

As the shadows of evening began to lengthen, Shirleen realized that the air was growing cooler. She worried now what the night would bring. Once the sun went down, temperatures plummeted, and often in the morning there were thick patches of frost atop everything.

When she had fallen to the ground after being hit over the head, her shawl and bonnet had fallen away from her. If she didn't die at the hands of these terrible renegades, the cold of night might take her life.

She looked ahead of her, and then behind her. She was the only survivor of the ambush. All of her friends had been murdered. She was now a captive, tied to a long length of rope with several Indian warriors who were captives as well.

Shirleen felt lucky to be alive and wondered why her life had been spared, but she could not help shuddering at the thought of what might lie ahead for her. She had seen how many of the renegades gazed hungrily at her. She expected to be raped when they stopped for the night.

And after they raped her, would she be killed? She would want to die of shame, yet she must live. She had her daughter to consider.

She turned her eyes straight ahead, her mind filled with thoughts that filled her with despair.

Megan!

Where was she?

Who was she with?

She knew Megan wasn't with the renegades, or she would have seen her.

So how had Megan gotten out of the fence? Shirleen had most definitely seen that it was closed when she allowed Megan to go outside to see the baby chicks.

Did that mean that although it had appeared to be shut, it really wasn't?

Oh, surely her husband hadn't latched it properly and her daughter had wandered out just prior to the Indian attack and was even now alone in the woods.

Or had the Indians come silently at first and stolen Megan away, and then made their attack?

But Shirleen didn't see how that was possible. She had not seen her daughter with any of the

Indians. That had to mean that even now Megan might be wandering alone, scared, and helpless.

The pain in the back of Shirleen's head, where the Indian had struck her with his war club, was almost unbearable.

But she did feel fortunate to be alive. The other women and children, her friends, had perished, and worse than that: She had awakened to a gruesome scene she would never forget . . . a scene of rape and scalping.

She had to get hold of herself and stop thinking about what had passed, and think of what would be. She must think about survival. She must think about her daughter's well-being.

And she could not help thinking about her feet. Oh, Lord, how they ached from walking so far, and she knew she surely had much farther to go before reaching these heathens' hideout.

There was only one hope that kept Shirleen sane: Surely someone would come along and see what was happening and try to stop the renegades!

Of course she knew that if someone did intervene, the chances were good that she would die during the ensuing battle. And not only she, but the other captives as well.

Truly puzzled that one red man would steal another red man, Shirleen looked over her shoulder at the captive Indians.

She noticed that many of them were scarred by smallpox and recalled how not long ago there had been an outbreak of the disease in the area.

When word had arrived that the deadly illness had struck the trading post, she and Earl and their friends had avoided going there for over a year.

Earl's current trip to the post was the first since they'd stopped their visits because of the smallpox. All the families in their small settlement were in dire need of necessities and had no choice now but to go and get the needed supplies.

Word had finally arrived that it was safe now to trade there.

It seemed the true danger had lain in staying home. No doubt the renegades had watched the men depart, leaving their families defenseless, and had waited long enough to make sure they would not return before attacking.

What puzzled her was why these pockmarked red men were among the captives. What could they have done to cause the renegades to take them captive?

Tears fell from her eyes as she again thought of her daughter and what might have happened to her. If Megan was out in the wilderness all alone, she might be the victim of animal attacks, or . . . other redskins.

She gazed heavenward and silently prayed that the good Lord would make all of these wrongs right, and look after her child, who was so pure and helpless.

Again she hung her head, her sore feet dragging even more heavily along the ground. Her legs were weak from walking so far without stopping to rest.

She reached up and found dried blood in her hair from her head injury, and a huge knot almost the size of a chicken egg.

It pounded as if someone were hitting her over and over again in the head with a hammer; the pain was so bad sometimes, she had the urge to vomit.

But she had thus far successfully kept herself from vomiting, for she was afraid that if she did, she might choke.

Her mouth was so dry. She couldn't remember when she had last had a drink of water.

Her stomach ached from hunger, so much that it felt as though something was twisting in her intestines.

No. She had never been so hungry, or thirsty, or afraid, as now. And she was so sad and empty at the loss of all of her friends. But worst of all was not knowing the fate of her lovely, sweet Megan.

All she could do was hope that her prayers reached the heavens and would be answered.

She wasn't sure how much longer she could last under these conditions, and the warriors seemed even more listless than she.

She tried to focus on something else. She wondered about her husband and the other men who were away trading. When they arrived home and discovered the massacre, what would they do?

Yes, she had planned to flee her husband today, but now she hoped that he cared enough to come and try to save her, although the scars on her back made by his belt proved the ugliness of his spirit. Perhaps she would be better off with Indians!

At least she knew that her husband cared enough about his daughter to search for her. He had never laid a hand on Megan. As far as Shirleen knew, Earl did truly love his daughter.

A movement to her far left, on a rise of land, drew Shirleen's attention suddenly. She saw a lone Indian there gazing down at those who were traveling below him. She wondered if he belonged to this renegade group, or another that might be even more heartless. Was he a scout of some kind?

By the way he turned to follow the procession down below him, it was certain that he had spotted her and the others.

She looked quickly ahead at the renegades and saw that they had not yet noticed the Indian who was spying on them. They were too cocky about their victory today, laughing and talking amongst themselves.

Her heart pounding, Shirleen gazed quickly up at the rise where she had seen the lone Indian, gasping when she saw he had disappeared.

The renegades continued to ride nonchalantly through the long, waving grass, unaware that they'd been seen.

She was not certain how to feel about that lone Indian. She did not know whether to feel hopeful that he and his friends might save her from the renegades who had come and raped and killed today.

Or should she fear them even more?

Thus far she had not been harmed by her captors except for the blow to her head.

Might these others rape her as soon as they had her as their captive?

Were they another band of renegades, or were they from a decent band of Indians?

Shirleen hoped for the latter. Perhaps they were a good-hearted band, who would let her go and search for her beloved Megan.

But knowing that most Indians hated white people because of what the white people had taken from them, Shirleen did not have much hope that she would be treated any better by a new group of Indians than she was now being treated.

Again she hung her head and walked dispiritedly through the grass, ignoring the splash of golden wildflowers at her far left. Usually she enjoyed seeing flowers. She would never hesitate to take a bouquet home for her supper table.

Tears filled her eyes again at the realization that her former life was now lost to her. She would no longer be among those who were civilized and God-loving.

Chapter Five

All our actions take their hues
From the complexion of the heart,
As landscapes their variety from light.

—Bacon

Blue Thunder rode down a steep slope to where his warriors and Gray Eyes awaited his return from scouting.

Knowing that it would be best for only one man to go spy on the travelers, Blue Thunder had chosen to ride alone to the top of the hill. He was eager to see if they had found Big Nose, and especially to see if he had red-skinned captives with him.

Blue Thunder knew the warriors from Gray Eyes' village as well as their own chief did because they met in joint council so often.

Blue Thunder was glad that he had not been seen by any of the renegades. He would have the element of surprise on his side when he chose to attack. Only one person had looked up at him, and that had been a white woman.

He had known instantly that she was the only survivor of the recent ambush.

He doubted that she would alert the Comanche renegades about having seen him.
Surely she was hoping that he would find a
way to help her as well as the other captives.

And . . . he . . . would!

As he rode onward to where his men and
Gray Eyes awaited his return in the darkest
shadows of a nearby forest, bitterness over-
whelmed him.

He would never forget the sight of Gray Eyes'
captured warriors tied in a long line along with
the lone white woman.

From his vantage point, on his steed on the
hill, he had not been able to pick out Big Nose
from the others, but he did know that those
were Big Nose's warriors.

Hatred for the Comanche renegade filled his
heart when he had looked more carefully at
Gray Eyes' captured warriors.

Some could barely stand, much less walk.

When one fell, another quickly helped him to
his feet.

Hardly able to bear the sight, Blue Thunder
had quickly shifted his gaze elsewhere, to the
one white captive.

After having seen the aftermath of the ambush, and the carnage left behind by the renegades, he wondered how this woman had
survived. What made her different from the others who had been left dead along the ground,
the women all heartlessly scalped and raped?

He could not seem to tear his thoughts from

the surviving white woman. She was a woman with flaming red hair, so tiny and vulnerable; yet she had walked with a lifted, proud chin.

She had not stumbled once while he watched her.

Now, as then, he got a sick feeling in the pit of his stomach when he thought of what her final fate would be at the hands of the Comanche renegades. She would eventually be passed around to all of the renegades, raped and tortured, and then killed.

His thoughts went suddenly to the white woman who lived in his village. She was a much different sort of woman in appearance from Big Nose's flame-haired captive. She was big-boned and strong.

Every time Blue Thunder thought about how she happened to live in his village, he could not help smiling, yet, in truth, he wished she was not a part of his people's lives.

Knowing this was not the time to be thinking about Speckled Fawn, he sank his heels into the flanks of his white steed and rode hard until he finally came to the spot where he had left his warriors and Gray Eyes.

He dismounted and led his horse into the dark shadows of the towering trees. Gray Eyes was waiting there, his expression eager.

"Who were the travelers that we heard?" Gray Eyes asked, his tone filled with anticipation.

Seeing Gray Eyes' warriors in his mind's eye again, how exhausted they were, stumbling along as the ropes yanked on them, Blue Thunder was suddenly hesitant to tell his friend what he had seen.

Yet he must, for each moment they waited before they went to rescue the men were moments that might bring death to one or more of them.

They were at the mercy of heartless renegades who murdered for the sheer pleasure of it.

"They were who we thought they might be," Blue Thunder said thickly. "The renegades have your warriors tied together by ropes. They are being forced to walk to their destination."

"Are they well enough, or are there signs they have been mistreated?" Gray Eyes asked, his eyes searching Blue Thunder's.

"My friend, from that distance it was hard to tell, but from what I could gather, some of your warriors are not well at all," Blue Thunder replied. "They have surely been beaten by their captors, but be thankful that at least these ones are alive. I would hate to think how many lie dead beside the trail."

A sudden rage rushed through Gray Eyes. His gaze narrowed and he doubled his hands into tight fists at his sides. "Big Nose will pay for this," he said tightly.

Then his eyes widened. "You did not say whether or not you saw Big Nose," he noted. "Was he among those who took my men captive?"

"No, I did not see him," Blue Thunder answered. "But I did not take the time to fully assess everything. We must act quickly in order to save those men who may not be able to go on much farther."

"Big Nose must be there, somewhere," Gray Eyes growled.

He placed a heavy hand on Blue Thunder's shoulder, then lowered it to his side. "What are we to do?" he asked, his voice filled with a harsh anger, which matched the fury in his eyes.

Blue Thunder motioned with a hand for his warriors to come and stand in a tight circle around him, while their horses munched lazily on grass beneath the trees.

"This is what we should do," Blue Thunder said, looking from one man to the other. "A group led by you, Gray Eyes, will circle around and come upon the renegades from one side, while another group led by me will attack from the other side. We will quickly pen in the renegades. They will have no choice but to surrender or die."

Each group was chosen.

The men hurried to their steeds.

With Gray Eyes in the lead, his assigned warriors went one way, while Blue Thunder and the warriors following his lead went another.

Blue Thunder rode hard as they made a wide circle until he and his men got so close they must proceed on foot, or the sound of the horses' hooves would alert the renegades that they were no longer alone.

Each carrying a loaded rifle, the warriors moved stealthily onward on foot, until they could hear the steady thudding of the renegades' horses' hooves.

They were so close now they could hear the groaning of those warriors who were in pain, warriors who might not live to see another tomorrow unless they were rescued and taken back to their village shaman.

From his vantage point, Blue Thunder could now see the white woman. She continued to walk courageously onward, her chin still held proudly high.

He had never wondered much about white women, except for the one who lived among his people. White women were a part of the white world, and he wanted nothing to do with it.

But this woman?

She was very different from those he had seen and observed. There was something so sweet and sensitive about her face as he observed her. Yet she was showing her strength and courage as she struggled to survive.

Blue Thunder was glad to be the one who would save her from captivity, for he wanted to know more about what made such a tiny thing as she behave so bravely.

He hoped that she had not witnessed the rapes and murders of the other white women, for that would make her hate and fear all red men, and he did not want her to hate him.

Ho, there was no doubt that he was intrigued by this tiny, flame-haired woman whose spirit surely matched the color of her hair.

Chapter Six

In what distant deeps or skies
Burnt the fire of thine eyes?

—Blake

Moments after circling the Comanche renegades, Blue Thunder shouted out a warning that they were surrounded and to give up their weapons as well as their captives. In the next instant, all hell seemed to break loose.

The renegades were not ready to give up so easily. They stopped and positioned their bows for firing, reaching back to grab arrows from their quivers.

Seeing this, and knowing that the Comanche would fight before giving themselves up, Blue Thunder shouted at the captives and white woman as he raised his rifle for firing. "Lie flat on the ground! Stay out of the line of fire!"

He had no time to see if they heeded his warning, for arrows began flying from the renegades' bows; the Assiniboine answered with more powerful weapons . . . their rifles.

As Blue Thunder shot first one renegade and then another, he was thankful that it seemed his warriors were more accurate with their shooting than the renegades. Not one of Blue Thunder's warriors fell from his steed, nor did Blue Thunder or Gray Eyes.

As the battle continued, Blue Thunder realized that Big Nose was not among the renegades. He must have fled like a coward before the attack. Perhaps he *had* noticed Blue Thunder scouting from the hill.

It seemed just the sort of thing the heartless man might do—save himself as those who followed him dutifully died fighting for him.

After the firing ceased, Blue Thunder realized that those renegades who were not killed had fled.

Miraculously, none of the captives, or those who'd come to save them had died.

The captives still lay prone on the ground, unsure of whether or not they were safe.

Blue Thunder and the men under his command quickly dismounted. Gray Eyes helped the captives up from the ground, reassuring them that they were finally safe from all harm, while Blue Thunder and his men went to the fallen renegades, lying in pools of their own blood, to make absolutely certain they were dead. In a matter of moments they had ascertained that none were alive.

Blue Thunder now turned to gaze at the white woman as she slowly sat up and returned his look.

Her true beauty was evident this close, but he also saw stark fear in her eyes. He was not surprised. She did not know one Indian from another and probably thought him and his warriors as dangerous as the Comanche renegades. After all, she had just seen them kill all the renegades who had not fled.

He returned her steady gaze and knew that this was not the time to reassure her that she was now safe and would be treated well. He knew that at this moment, while death lay all around her, anything he said to her would be wasted words, for he doubted she would believe him.

He turned and watched Gray Eyes gather around him those of his warriors who were strong enough to stand and listen.

His heart swelled with pride and love for Gray Eyes as his friend went from one man to another, taking the time to hug and reassure each.

Blue Thunder could well imagine the pain his friend was feeling in his heart when Gray Eyes went to those warriors who could hardly hold their heads up from the ground.

Gray Eyes hugged each of them, reassuring them that all would now be well.

Once he had explained the debt of gratitude they all owed Blue Thunder, all who could stand gathered with Blue Thunder's warriors and awaited orders from Blue Thunder and Gray Eyes about what their next move might be.

"Go through the bags that the Comanche have placed on their packhorses. Inside will be

the belongings they stole from the white people's cabins before burning them," Blue Thunder said, slowly looking from man to man.

Gray Eyes was standing back a little, giving
Blue Thunder the right to direct all the men.

Gray Eyes found himself fighting back tears,
so he would not look weak in the eyes of his
friend. He owed Blue Thunder so much for
what he had risked today . . . the chance that
his own men might die for the sake of those
who belonged to another Assiniboine band.

"Also round up all of the horses—not only
those that belonged to the downed renegades,
but also those that were stolen from the herd
of the Owl Band," Blue Thunder said. "Take
them back to your homes. You also will share
the white people's possessions and horses that
we have made our own."

Gray Eyes stepped up to Blue Thunder. "The
horses that the Comanche stole from me and
those that belonged to the white people are
now yours, my friend, as well as the bags of
the white people's belongings. These all shall
be yours in thanks for what you did for me and
my warriors today."

Before Blue Thunder could argue the point
with Gray Eyes, his friend walked a few steps
past Blue Thunder and closely studied the
white woman.

He then turned to Blue Thunder again. "I do
not ask for the white woman," he said thickly.
"My friend, will you take her? White women are
helpless and unable to do the work of Indian

women. This woman would only eat food necessary for my own people's survival. Blue Thunder, you have food enough to share with this captive, as well as lodging and pelts to keep her warm when the cold winter winds begin to blow. I have lost so much. I do not need a white woman to take what little we have left."

Blue Thunder hesitated. He had never wanted captives of any sort, especially those with white skin. He had no wish to give the white pony soldiers cause to come to his village because a white woman was there.

But . . . this was not just any white woman. He had seen enough of her to know that she was someone who intrigued him to the very core of his being.

And knowing that what his friend had said was true, Blue Thunder was tempted to agree to his offer of handing the white woman over to him.

"I see what you say as true, and because I do not want to see any more harm come to your village, I will take her myself. If her presence brings white pony soldiers to the Wind Band, I have enough warriors to discourage an attack," Blue Thunder said. He nodded as he took slow steps toward Shirleen, his gaze never leaving her green eyes. "Yes, I will take her."

Shirleen trembled as Blue Thunder stepped up to her, his eyes still reaching into her soul, it seemed.

There was much about this powerful-looking Indian that told her he was not one to fear, yet it was still true that his skin was red, and red-skinned men had come and destroyed her world today. They had brutally murdered her neighbors, people who'd never brought harm into anyone's lives. They were all God-loving souls.

She swallowed hard as she fought back the sting of tears at the thought of her sweet Megan. She was almost certain now that she would never see or hold her daughter again.

She felt so numb inside, she no longer cared whether she was a captive or not.

As far as she was concerned, her life was over. She was the same as dead, for everything within her told her that life was no longer worth living.

All the same, she tensed when Blue Thunder stepped closer to her.

He reached out and spread her blood-stiffened hair to study her wound. His shaman would make it well, and then Blue Thunder would set the woman free, so she could find her way back to her own world.

There were forts close by his village. He would take her near one, then set her free to go the rest of the way on her own.

After she was healed by the shaman and cared for by Blue Thunder's people, surely she would not go to the fort and complain about him. He was the one who had saved her.

Surely she knew this, even though she was looking at him as though he were one of those whom had killed and raped.

He would give her time enough to know the truth about him and his people before setting her free. She would in time realize that he had saved her from a fate worse than death.

"*Hakamya-upo*. In my language I tell you to come with me," Blue Thunder explained in English, placing a gentle hand at Shirleen's elbow. He understood when she yanked herself away from him, her eyes filled with a sudden loathing.

"Come with me," Blue Thunder insisted, stepping toward her as she backed farther away from him. "I mean you no harm. I am a friend. I have rescued you from the renegades. I will take you to my village and see that your wound is cared for. I will give you clean clothes. I will give you food. I will also give you a lodge of your own until the time comes for you to go on your way again."

"I want freedom *now*," Shirleen blurted out. "I . . . do . . . not want to go with you. Not anywhere."

"If you do not come with me, other renegades will find you. You would not even want to think what your fate would be then," Blue Thunder said softly.

"You are only trying to frighten me," Shirleen accused, her voice breaking.

"Yes, I am, especially if that is the only way I can get you to go with me," Blue Thunder said. "You are with friends. You will not be harmed while you are in my company."

"And I am to believe that?" Shirleen said, laughing sarcastically.

"In time you will see the truth of what I say," Blue Thunder replied, reaching out and taking her gently by the hand. "Now come. It is time to start back toward my home."

Recalling how viciously the renegades had killed and raped her friends, and noticing that this warrior's words were spoken kindly and sincerely, Shirleen knew that for now she had no better choice than to go with him.

She shyly nodded.

After she was placed on a horse, she slowly looked around her. The Indians had gathered the stolen horses together, as well as those with the bags of clothes on them.

She made it a point not to gaze at the fallen, bloody renegades, although she was glad they were dead.

All she wanted for now was to get away from this horrible place and find some sort of sanity in what remained of her life.

It all seemed like a bad dream she might never awaken from!

Chapter Seven

Act well at the moment,
And you have performed
A good action to all eternity.

—Lovater

Shirleen could hardly believe her good fortune. She was riding one of the horses that the Comanche had stolen from her friends. The familiarity of the steed was especially welcome since everything else was vastly different from the life she'd known before.

She had been told by the chief of these Indians that she was no longer a captive, but someone who had been rescued.

She would believe it only when she was truly released to try to put her life back together.

She knew her life would never be the same. Her daughter was gone, and Shirleen had been left with the hideous memory of the deaths of her special friends.

She could hardly believe that her life had been spared, but surely it had been for a purpose. To find and save her daughter from harm.

In time, oh, if the good Lord was willing, she would be able to fulfill that purpose.

Her head was pounding so hard she found it difficult to hold it up as she continued riding beside the chief, but she did. She didn't want to look weak in the eyes of these Indians, or they might come to the conclusion that she was not worth the trouble of helping and would leave her behind.

But she had seen how the chief had given her occasional sideways glances.

She supposed he was looking at her like this to see if she was alright and still able to make the journey to his village.

Yet there was something else in his eyes when she happened to meet his gaze. It was nothing akin to the loathing she had thought all Indians felt for white people.

Instead, there was a kindness, a softness in his dark eyes that made her believe she was in the company of someone she could trust.

And there was something else in his eyes that filled her with wonder. He was gazing at her as if she were someone he truly cared for, as though they were not strangers, but instead kindred spirits. She, too, was feeling something vastly different from hate for this red man. She actually felt intrigued by him.

And how could she not?

She had never seen such a handsome man in her entire life. His facial features were sculpted to perfection. His long, black hair, which reached far down his straight, muscular back, was beautiful and shone beneath the rays of the sun as though he had just come from bathing in the river.

And as his hair fluttered when a breeze swept through it, she could almost smell its cleanness. She could almost feel it against the palms of her hands.

How different this man was from her husband. Earl had worn his hair long, too, but it was blond, not shining blue-black. And Earl's hair had never smelled good.

Then, too, the chief was tall, his body fully muscled. It filled out his fringed buckskins to perfection.

She blushed when she wondered how it would feel to run her hands down the chief's muscled back.

She had been repelled by the very nearness of Earl's body after she realized the sort of man he was.

It had gotten so that just being near Earl made her want to vomit.

And Earl was a man who scarcely bathed.

The smell of perspiration that always clung to him and his clothes had made her stay as far from him as she could. She had dreaded those times when he would grab her and almost wrestle her to the bed before taking what he wanted from her . . . even in the presence of their precious daughter.

It was so good to know that that would never

happen again; nor would she ever have to look into his leering blue eyes as he forced himself on her.

Her thoughts of Earl were interrupted when up ahead, in a clearing of trees, she saw many tepees nestled beside a beautiful river. A bluff reached out high above them on the far side of the village.

And as she grew closer and was able to see the whole camp, she noticed how clean the tepees were, and how smoke spiraled slowly from their smoke holes.

She even smelled the delicious aroma of meat cooking, which caused hunger pangs in the pit of her stomach.

She only now realized just how long it had been since she had eaten. Not since early this morning when she had made oats and fried eggs for herself and Megan.

When Megan came to mind again, tears filled Shirleen's eyes. She prayed that her child was alive somewhere and being treated kindly. But she feared that could not be, especially if she was with the damnable Comanche renegades.

She had heard mention of Big Nose among the Indians who had rescued her. Surely he was the one they had truly wanted to find and kill.

Before she had been hit over the head with a war club, she remembered having seen a renegade with a strange-looking bulbous nose, with purple veins running in all directions across it.

Just as she was hit, he had looked at her and smiled cruelly.

Oh, Lord, if that man had her daughter . . . !

Again her thoughts were interrupted, and she was glad, for she did not like where they had taken her.

It was best not to labor over her daughter's misfortune.

Not now, anyway. There was nothing at all she could do for the present.

But when she was well enough to ride a long distance, she would not stop until she found her daughter. And although Shirleen was not skilled with firearms, she would use one to rescue Megan if need be.

Now they had arrived in the midst of the village, where women and children and many elderly people stopped to stare at her. Shirleen kept her eyes locked straight ahead. She was afraid to look into the eyes of those who lived in the village, for she was white, and most whites were hated by Indians.

Most warriors who had stayed behind paid her no heed, but watched their chief until he drew rein before the largest tepee in the village.

Blue Thunder dismounted and smiled at the warriors who greeted him, then nodded toward the edge of the village, where the rescued horses were being led into a corral.

"Go. There are many captured horses," he said. "Divide them among yourselves."

When the men looked questioningly at him,

he added, "Our mission was successful. Our friend Gray Eyes' stolen warriors are soon to be reunited with their families."

"And what of Big Nose?" one of the warriors asked anxiously. "Has he been stopped forever?"

Blue Thunder kneaded his chin, gazed down at the ground, then raised his eyes slowly again. "He was not among the fallen renegades," he said, regretting that he had lost the opportunity to question Big Nose about Shawnta's death. "Somehow he escaped our wrath. But he will be brought to justice one day. I promise you that."

He noticed how his warriors' eyes now went to Shirleen, then turned again to him in question.

"I have not brought a captive white woman among us," Blue Thunder said, going to Shirleen and helping her from the horse.

He gently placed a hand at her elbow and walked her closer to the men, who were now being joined by women and children. "This woman was being forced into captivity by Big Nose and his renegades," he said softly.

"Why have you brought her among us?" one of the warriors asked.

"And how long will she be with us?" one of the women asked quickly.

"She is here only for our shaman to see to her wound. She was injured on her head by the renegades," Blue Thunder said, indicating the dried blood in Shirleen's hair. "She survived the wound, but it needs medicine so that it will completely heal."

He gazed at the woman who had asked the question about how long Shirleen would be among them. "She will stay only long enough for her wound to heal, and then she will be free to go," he said, yet his heart was not in his words.

He felt protective of her and even more than that.

His fascination with her had aroused needs that he had not allowed himself to feel while in the presence of any woman, white or red-skinned, since the death of his precious wife, Shawnta. Since her death, he had put all his energy into fulfilling his duties as chief.

But now?

He was beginning to feel the need to have a woman in his life again.

And if it was this white woman who sparked such need, so be it!

But he now had to make her understand that she was safe among his people. And the fact that he no longer saw resentment or hate in her eyes made him hope that he might be able to reach inside her heart.

"Come with me," Blue Thunder said as he led Shirleen away from everyone. "After I decided to bring you to my village, I sent a warrior ahead to make certain a tepee was prepared for you. It is not as fancy as you are probably accustomed to in your white world, but it should be comfortable enough for you as you recover from the head wound."

Shirleen was struck anew by his kindness, by his gentleness toward her.

He took her by the elbow and led her past his tepee to a beautiful lodge set at a little distance from the others. It was much smaller than his, but it was enough for her.

Blue Thunder held aside the entrance flap. He nodded toward the opening. Not at all afraid or apprehensive, Shirleen stepped lightly past him.

Just inside the tepee, she stopped and gazed around her. It was most certainly smaller than the others she had seen in the village, and there was nothing in the tepee, only an earthen floor and rocks positioned in a circle of dug-out earth in the middle of the tepee. The rocks were situated beneath a smoke hole, so she knew that this must be the Indian firepit she had heard about.

Suddenly she realized that she was alone. While she had been so absorbed in looking around her, the man who had brought her there had left the tepee.

She heard his voice just outside the entrance. He was telling one of his warriors in English to stand guard outside her lodge.

Suddenly she no longer felt so much at ease. Why was she being guarded?

She had heard tales of Indian captives, and she shivered at the thought of what usually happened to those captive women.

But then she recalled how he had said she would be among these people for only the length of time that it would take for her injury to heal. Once her strength returned, she would be allowed to leave.

But now she wondered if he had only told her that to make her cooperate with his plans.

She badly wanted to ask the young chief to search for Megan, but knew now that she must be careful about everything she said to him. First she must see if he was truthful; she must judge how he treated her. If what he had told her were lies, she would not even mention Megan's plight, for he would be of no help.

Standing quietly in the tepee, now no longer hearing the young chief talking with the warrior who stood outside the entrance, Shirleen was not sure what she should do. There were no comforts at all in the tepee, not even a blanket upon which to sit.

At that moment, two Indian maidens came into the lodge. One immediately spread what looked like bulrush mats over the earthen floor, leaving none of the ground exposed to the naked eye, while the other woman brought in firewood and started a fire in the firepit.

They left, but soon returned again. One carried blankets. The other positioned a pot of tantalizing-smelling food over the fire, hanging it from a tripod of sorts.

They left again, and before Shirleen could have time to wonder about all that was happening, the women returned.

One carried a wooden basin of water, the other wooden bowls and spoons.

The two women wore beautifully beaded doe-skin dresses and matching moccasins, their coal-black hair hanging in long braids down their backs. They said nothing to Shirleen, nor did she say anything to them.

And then she was left alone again.

She turned and watched the entrance flap, expecting the women to return with other things. But this time it seemed that they were gone for good.

She was glad to be alone, for her head was throbbing again where she had been struck by the horrible club. Groaning with pain, she sank to the mats beside the warm fire.

She hung her face in her hands and sobbed, then stopped when she heard someone enter the tepee.

Afraid of who it might be, she looked slowly up and saw an intelligent-looking old man standing there with a buckskin bag.

The Indian spoke to her in good English.

"I am called by the name Morning Thunder," he said in a deep, resonant tone. "I am my people's shaman, which in your white world is called a doctor. I have come at the command of my chief Blue Thunder to see to your wound."

Unsure of how to feel about this old man's presence, Shirleen sat up stiffly and looked at him anxiously.

"Do not be afraid," Morning Thunder said softly as he knelt down on the mats, gently turning Shirleen to face him. "You are with a friendly band of Assiniboine people who do not kill whites unless forced into it."

Shirleen swallowed hard. "I am no danger to any of you," she said. "I will do nothing to cause you to want me dead."

Morning Thunder smiled, reached out, and gently separated her hair to check the wound.

He "tsk-tsk'd," as Shirleen remembered her grandmother doing so often when she was not pleased with something.

The familiar sound made Shirleen relax.

"It hurts so much," she offered.

"I shall take the pain away," Morning Thunder reassured her. "Close your eyes as I tend to your wound if it will make you feel better. Soon my healing powers will make you well."

Shirleen was surprised that she had been in the presence of two powerful Indians, and both had shown her kindness.

And more than that. She was so glad to know that she was with a friendly tribe of Indians, the Assiniboine.

She was beginning to hope that the young chief, who she now knew was called Blue Thunder, was sincere in what he had said to her.

"You are called by what name?" Morning Thunder asked as he slowly and carefully washed Shirleen's wound, removing all the blood.

"Shirleen," she responded without hesitation. She felt comfortable in his presence, and he was as gentle as her grandmother and mother had been when she had gotten hurt as a child.

This had been a frequent occurrence, because of her size; everyone always got the better of her in the rougher sorts of games.

She had preferred jump rope or jacks, games that would not cause her harm, or dirty her pretty dresses.

"I believe you should be called Tiny Flames," Morning Thunder said as he stopped and admired her red hair, which reminded him of the color of flame. "While you are in my presence, I shall always address you by your Indian name."

Shirleen's eyes widened with pleasure at being given an Indian name . . . and one that was so beautiful!

She hoped that Morning Thunder's kindness wasn't part of a scheme to make her relax so she would be a more compliant prisoner. She did want to trust those who had made kind overtures toward her, especially Blue Thunder.

"I love the name," Shirleen murmured, blushing slightly when she noticed him studying her face. "Thank you."

"In my tongue you thank someone by saying *pila-maye*," Morning Thunder explained, smiling at her as he set aside the cloth that he had used to wash the blood from her hair.

"*Pila-maye*," Shirleen murmured. "I will try to remember the correct words in your tongue when I have a reason to thank someone."

"You will have many reasons, for my people are going to be nothing but kind to you," Morning Thunder said, now applying a white medicinal powder to her wound. "As I am being kind to you today, I shall also be kind tomorrow."

Shirleen stiffened when the powder he was applying to her wound caused a pain to shoot through her scalp.

"It will hurt for only a little while, and then the true healing begins," Morning Thunder said as he drew his hand away from her head.

"You are so very kind," Shirleen murmured. "I will always remember your kindness."

"And I will remember your soft sweetness," Morning Thunder said, his eyes smiling into hers as she blushed.

She was feeling less and less apprehensive about being in the Assiniboine village, especially now that she believed that these Indians truly wanted to help her.

Now if she could only find Megan!

Chapter Eight

So sweet the blush of bashfulness,
Even pity scarce can wish it less.

—Byron

Alone and now dressed comfortably in a clean
doeskin gown that the shaman had given her,
Shirleen sat on a soft pallet of blankets beside
the fire in the tepee that had been assigned
her. Physically, she was feeling better since
Morning Thunder had medicated her wound.

But tears filled her eyes, for she had never
felt as alone and desperate as now.

Yes, she had gone through some rough times
with her husband Earl, but nothing compared
to being captured by renegades and separated
from her precious daughter.

She was beginning to fear that she would
never know Megan's fate, even if she went to a
fort after she left the Indian village and reported her loss to the colonel in charge. Out
there in the West, one could disappear and
never be heard of again.

That was one thing that had frightened her

when Earl had talked of moving to Wyoming, yet at the time, he was behaving normally and protectively toward her, so she had put her trust in him. She had believed he would protect her and had left Boston without so much as a look back over her shoulder.

It had been exciting to think of going to a new land, where she and Earl would build a home and have children.

She had felt proud to be creating a home of her own. Before she had met and married Earl, she'd scarcely left her parents' home, except for an occasional social function with her parents and their friends.

She had not even joined the other girls her age to go to parties, where she heard they danced the night away in beautiful gowns in the arms of handsome partners.

Although many young men had wanted to come courting, enthralled by her sweetness and beauty, she had not had the desire to receive any of them inside her heart.

She had been content spending time alone in her bedroom, reading books and dreaming of things that surely would never be.

She had at times even dreamed of coming face-to-face with a handsome Indian after reading novels about life out West.

It seemed strange that she was actually living that dream, only now it was filled with too much grief to be anything like her girlish fantasies.

She had thought when she'd met Earl that he might be her only chance of seeing what the

West was truly like. When he had come to her home to visit her father with talk of business affairs, she had heard him mention that he had a dream of one day moving out West. At those words, she had been instantly intrigued by him.

She had willingly accepted his first invitation to go to dinner . . . and there it had begun.

Just the thought of being free and moving to a new land with a new husband had been so exciting, Shirleen had sometimes felt sick to her stomach. In those days, excitement had caused her body to react in such a way.

Now?

She had not had anything to get excited about for some time, except for when she had started planning her escape with her daughter.

Of course, fear had been mixed in with that excitement, for she had never been on her own under any circumstances.

She had never been the master of her own destiny.

Not even now, unless what the young chief said was true, and that she could leave when she felt strong enough to do so.

As it was now, when she tried to stand, she got dizzy.

But otherwise, she felt much better. She had been cared for so gently by the shaman, and had been given such a nice, soft gown to wear, since her own clothes had been ruined by all the blood.

The aroma of the food cooking over the fire

made her belly suddenly growl. Trusting that the food in the pot over the fire was edible, even if the ingredients might be strange to her, she grabbed the empty wooden bowl and reached for the ladle that rested in the food.

Though she did not recognize any of the vegetables, or know what kind of meat floated amid them, she ladled a bowl full. Then she sat back down and grabbed up a spoon that had also been brought to her, and ate ravenously.

She didn't stop until a surprising visitor appeared at the entrance to her tepee. She was stunned to see that it was a white woman who wore a beautifully beaded doeskin dress and matching moccasins, her long, blond hair worn in a lone braid down her back.

"I have come to talk with you. May I enter?" the woman asked, questioning Shirleen with her eyes.

"Yes, I guess so," Shirleen mumbled, her eyes widening as the woman came and sat down beside her.

Shirleen was astonished to see another white woman in the Assiniboine village. This woman seemed content to be dressed as an Indian squaw, and was evidently allowed to come and go as she pleased.

A sudden disturbing thought came to Shirleen. She had heard about powerful Indian chiefs taking white women as wives; could this woman be Chief Blue Thunder's wife?

But she just could not imagine those two together. The woman was older and not all that pretty. She was big–boned and fleshy.

"I am Speckled Fawn," the other woman said, smiling at Shirleen. "I see that you are surprised to see another white woman in this village. I'm sure you are wondering why I am here."

No longer hungry for food, but instead for information, Shirleen set her half-empty bowl aside. "Yes, I do want to know who you are," she said guardedly as she gazed into the bluest eyes she had ever seen. They were even bluer than her husband's and her daughter's. "Why are you here? Clearly you are no captive, for you are free to come and go as you please."

Shirleen leaned toward the woman. "Why have you come to see me? Were you made to come and talk with me?" she blurted out. "Is it a part of the young chief's ploy to make me feel more at ease among his people?"

"Chief Blue Thunder is not a scheming man," Speckled Fawn said softly. "He is perhaps the kindest man I have ever known."

"Are you . . . his . . . wife?" Shirleen blurted out. As soon as the words left her mouth, she wished she hadn't asked the woman such a question. The last thing she wanted to do was betray her keen interest in the handsome chief.

"I am married to an Indian of this village, but not to Blue Thunder," Speckled Fawn said.

"Blue Thunder has no wife," Speckled Fawn went on. "He did, but . . ."

Not wanting to think of the woman who'd been so kind to her, and who was now dead because of the renegades, Speckled Fawn quickly changed the subject.

"I have come here to assure you that you are among friends," Speckled Fawn said. "These people are of the Assiniboine tribe. You are very fortunate to have been rescued by them, as was I."

"You . . . too . . . ?" Shirleen asked, her eyes widening.

"Yes. I have been here for some time now and enjoy my life as never before," Speckled Fawn said, smiling at Shirleen. "I have come to do what I can to make your time here more pleasant. The first thing I will do is take you to the pile of clothes that were brought to the village after Blue Thunder and his warriors took them from the Comanche renegades. Surely among those clothes are some that you will want. Unfortunately, the things you had on when you were injured are not fit to be worn again. The bloodstains on them are permanent."

Speckled Fawn paused and smiled at Shirleen. "I understand why you might be afraid to trust anyone in this village," she said. "I was afraid, too, when I first arrived here. I had heard horrible tales of how white women were mistreated by Indians. Well, it did not take long for me to learn that the Indians at this village would be far kinder to me than anyone in the white community. My family was slaughtered on their way to Wyoming, and I was forced to do anything that I could to survive . . . things I am not proud of having done."

She paused, sucked in a nervous breath, then continued. "I had been a dance hall queen, and sometimes even worse than that, but circumstances occurred to change that part of my life," Speckled Fawn said solemnly. "I won't go into what those circumstances were, but just that I wandered alone and was near death when I was found by the Assiniboine Indians and brought to this village. I have now been here for five summers, which in the white way of describing things is five years. I was married shortly after my arrival to a man of this village, and I have never been happier."

As Shirleen listened to what the woman told her, she saw just how happy she did seem to be. Yet Shirleen was not ready to open up and discuss her own life with this woman who was a total stranger to her.

Who was to say if what the woman told her was truth? Perhaps she was just toying with Shirleen, or even jealous that another white woman was now in the village.

"What is your name?" Speckled Fawn asked softly. "Surely you will share at least that with me, for I am here as a friend, and the only other white person in the village."

Still Shirleen said nothing, yet she was thinking of the Indian name she had been given by the shaman. It had a beautiful sound to it.

Tiny Flames.

Yes, if she had to be called something while she was in this village, she wished to be known as Tiny Flames.

But Shirleen wasn't ready to share even that much with this white woman, not until she knew whether her friendly overtures were genuine.

Speckled Fawn got to her feet. "If you don't want to tell me your name, that's fine and dandy," she said, shrugging. "But please come with me to sort through the clothes."

Shirleen quickly shook her head, refusing to do anything this woman asked her to do.

"I understand," Speckled Fawn said softly. "Well, by gum, if you won't go with me, I'll bring some clothes to you."

Speckled Fawn left and soon returned with a huge bag.

Shirleen's eyes widened as the woman dumped the clothes out on the mats that covered the earthen floor.

She gasped when she saw that many of the clothes had belonged to her and her daughter. Her eyes lingered on one of Megan's dresses, which Shirleen had made only recently. Each stitch had been taken with the deepest love. When Megan had put it on, she'd been so delighted by the embroidered flowers on the collar, she had swirled around and around, giggling. It was a special moment between mother and daughter that was their very own.

She suddenly thought of the sweater she had

put on Megan this morning. Megan had even
tried to put a few stitches of embroidery on the
front herself, since Shirleen was sewing baby
chickens on it. She'd wanted to make it extra
special for her daughter since Megan loved
baby chickens so much.

Recalling the sight of Megan rushing outside
with the sweater on to play with the baby
chicks, Shirleen felt tears prick her eyes. She
hoped it would keep Megan warm at night
wherever she was.

She swallowed hard as she fought her
doubts that Megan was even still alive.

"May I be alone?" Shirleen suddenly asked,
picking up Megan's tiny dress and holding it to
her breast. "Please?"

"Yes, I'll leave," Speckled Fawn said, already
turning to walk toward the entrance.

She stopped and turned and gazed into
Shirleen's eyes again. "But while I am gone,
please choose the clothes you want to keep, for
the rest will be divided among the women of
this village."

Shirleen nodded and waited breathlessly to
again be totally alone. She needed this time to
think of a way to discover the whereabouts of
her daughter.

But . . . how . . . ?

Chapter Nine

There is nothing held so dear as love,
If only it be hard to win.

—Ingelow

Deep in thought about what she had just experienced with the stranger who had been brought into the village, Speckled Fawn stepped into the tepee she shared with her Indian husband.

She stopped before going farther, her mind struck by something that had just transpired in the other tepee.

It was the woman's reaction to seeing a child's dress.

It was the reaction of a mother who longed for her child!

Did the woman's reaction mean that the dress belonged to her daughter? But if so, where was she?

And why wouldn't the woman share even her name with Speckled Fawn? Surely she had seen that Speckled Fawn had come to visit her as a friend.

But still . . . the woman had only spoken when Speckled Fawn had first arrived at the tepee. Otherwise she had remained silent, except at the last, when she'd plucked the child's dress from the other clothes.

Yes, the tiny dress had prompted the woman to react, surely evoking memories that pained her.

Yet no one had said anything about a small child, a girl, being among those who had been killed by the renegades.

Was the woman's daughter even now at the mercy of Big Nose and the evil men who had managed to flee the ambush by Blue Thunder and his warriors?

Realizing that eyes were on her, Speckled Fawn looked quickly down at her husband, who sat beside the fire, a blanket wrapped around his thin, slumped shoulders.

When he smiled somewhat blankly at her, Speckled Fawn's heart felt a warmth and depth of love she had never known she could feel for a man. Especially a man who was elderly, and who no longer had the ability to speak.

He now sat, day in and day out, awaiting his time to die, so that he could join his beloved ancestors in the sky.

But until then, Speckled Fawn did everything humanly possible to make him happy.

She believed that he was still alive only because she was there to love and care for him.

She just wished that he could talk, and still had the capacity to reason, because she badly wished to talk to him about the white woman, and especially her reaction to the tiny dress. She would love to know his opinion on the situation.

But as it was, she could only tell him of her feelings, which she often did in order to make him feel that he was still involved in life. She spoke even though she knew that he could never talk back to her.

"My husband, I've returned home to sit with you, to talk and make you happy," Speckled Fawn said to Dancing Shadow. At one time, when he was younger and had his full faculties, he had been his people's shaman.

Speckled Fawn noticed that, as usual, her words had not registered, for his eyes had already turned away from her and he was again only watching the leaping flames of the fire in the firepit.

Used to this reaction, but never liking it any more than the last time she had tried to break through his terrible silence, Speckled Fawn sighed heavily.

She sat down beside him and took one of his bony hands in hers. She held it, feeling its coldness even though he was sitting close to the warmth of the fire.

Too often of late he felt cold when she touched him, especially when she bathed him each morning.

His chest, which was now strangely caved in

so that his ribs were prominent, held no warmth whatsoever, nor did his lips when she kissed him.

It was like kissing a dead fish. . . .

That thought made her shudder. She no longer wanted to kiss him because of how his lips felt against hers, but she hoped that perhaps a kiss might reach his consciousness, so she did it as often as she could.

"My husband, our chief returned today from his journey to find and kill Big Nose and his renegade friends," Speckled Fawn murmured. Her words would reach the fire, the walls of the tepee, the mats on the floor, even the pot of food cooking slowly over the fire, but not her husband's mind.

But still, she talked, for she knew that it was important not to leave her husband in total silence.

She kept hoping for some sort of breakthrough.

If he would say one word, it would cause her heart to leap with pure joy!

"Sad to say, though, Big Nose once again eluded death," Speckled Fawn said, herself now gazing into the fire. It had a way of almost hypnotizing a person, so she turned her eyes back to her husband. "He even eluded Blue Thunder. But most of Big Nose's men were killed. At least in that, your nephew can be proud."

She looked over her shoulder at the closed

entrance flap when she heard voices as someone walked past.

They were women, surely discussing the
events that had happened today in their village, the most shocking being the arrival of the
other white woman.

Many of these women had accepted Speckled Fawn's presence, but there were those who
still resented her, especially since one of their
most precious elders had taken her as his wife.

Dancing Shadow had chosen Speckled Fawn
as his wife soon after she had been brought
into the village.

At that time he had still had his senses
about him.

He had even given her her Indian name.

Some days after their marriage vows had
been spoken, her husband had fallen into his
strange life of silence.

They had never shared intimacy of the sort
husbands and wives normally shared.

But he had had a few nights of just being
able to enjoy the warmth of his wife next to
him in bed.

He had never once touched her intimate
parts. Nor had he even gazed at her when she
was undressed. He had given her all the privacy she could have wished for.

That pleased Speckled Fawn, for after what
she had gone through the weeks and months
before her rescue by Blue Thunder, she felt
nothing but loathing for men!

She was so glad she did not feel that way any longer. While among these Assiniboine people, no man among them had looked at her with lust, or treated her unjustly.

She was the wife of a wonderful old man.

She was treated with respect because of who her husband was, and had been.

"Husband, I am no longer the only white woman in our village," Speckled Fawn confided. "There was a horrible massacre of white people by Big Nose and his men. All the white people who were attacked died except one. It was a woman. She was brought to our village. Her wound has been treated by Morning Thunder, and she now sits in a tepee that Blue Thunder assigned her. She is not a true captive, though. When she is well enough to travel, she will leave us."

She reached a hand to her husband's chin and slowly turned his face toward her, but still there was no recognition of her, or of anything that she had just told him.

She let go of his face so that he could look into the fire again.

She often wondered what he saw.

Did he see some of his past flickering before his eyes as the flames danced and popped and zigzagged along the pile of wood?

Or did he truly see nothing at all?

"Husband, the woman seems so lost, so deeply hurt inside her heart over what has happened to her at the hands of the renegades," Speckled Fawn went on. Despite his lack of response, she believed that somehow these moments with her were important to her husband.

Otherwise he would be alone, totally alone, in his silent world.

Feeling blessed to have been chosen by him to be his wife, knowing how powerful he had once been, Speckled Fawn was happy to give her husband all the respect and love that were due him.

She would remain by his side until the end.

Once he took his last breath, he would finally be among those he surely thought of all day, even though he was no longer able to express what, or whom, he was thinking about.

It was those brief moments when he gave Speckled Fawn a fleeting smile that made her certain he somehow did hear her when she spoke to him, and fully appreciated her nearness.

"My husband, something just happened while I was with the white woman to make me think she might have a daughter," Speckled Fawn said softly. "It was the way she held a tiny dress taken from the white settlement that was attacked. But where is the child? Who might she be with?"

She swallowed hard. "I so fear she is with Big Nose," she said tightly. "He might have separated her from the others and taken her away before Blue Thunder's attack. Oh, God be with her if she is with that demon."

She slid her hand from his and brushed a

fallen lock of his hair back from his brow. "I wish the woman would confide in me," she said thickly. "As it is, she doesn't trust me. I imagine it's because I am white and living among your people and am dressed like your women. I would have had the same reaction five years ago had I found a white woman among your people when I was brought here."

She saw that a corner of her husband's blanket had slid from his shoulder.

She leaned closer to him and repositioned the blanket so that it would warm his aged, wrinkled flesh.

"My husband, I want to go and meet with Blue Thunder, to tell him about the white woman's reaction to the tiny dress, but I'm not sure if he will agree to meet with me," she said, her voice catching. "Although I have never done anything to cause Blue Thunder to despise me, he still seems to. I am aware that he has never approved of my being here. He never wanted me to marry you, his people's shaman, and also his uncle. But since I am your wife, I have been tolerated by not only him, but also by the men of our village. Thank goodness I have made friends with most of the women."

When Dancing Shadow slowly turned his gaze to her, he looked deep into her eyes. Since he usually looked at her blankly, she sensed that this time he had understood at least a portion of what she had just said.

She frowned, thinking that if he understood there were some who still did not appreciate her living among them, the knowledge would hurt his heart. She had to be more careful about what she said, just in case he did understand but could not speak his mind to react to what he heard.

When he turned his eyes away from her and hung his head, quickly falling asleep where he sat, Speckled Fawn reached out for him and helped him down onto his pallet of blankets and furs beside the fire.

She positioned a rich pelt from a red fox beneath his head, his long hair spreading over it like a gray halo, then slowly covered him.

"My husband, oh, my husband, I so wish there was something I could do for you that you would feel and know," she whispered. She brushed a soft kiss across his leathery brow. "I love you. Oh, at least please know how much I love and adore you. You have given me such peace inside my heart. I will be lost without you when you are taken from me."

She leaned away from him, filled with gratitude for this elderly man. Without his attention toward her, who could say where she might be now, or with whom?

She had no idea whether or not Blue Thunder would have asked her to stay with his people if she were not Dancing Shadow's wife.

But she was, and she knew that even if her husband passed on to the other side, she would still live among the Assiniboine, for she would be the widow of one of the most powerful shamans in Assiniboine history.

At least that was what she had been told.

Stubborn by nature, and unable to get the white woman off her mind, Speckled Fawn decided to go back and talk some more to her.

The other woman seemed to have lost everything that was precious to her. It was a plight Speckled Fawn recognized all too well. She had felt the same way, had lost just as much the day her wagon train was ambushed and her parents lost their lives.

Chapter Ten

Beauty is truth, truth beauty—
That is all ye know on earth,
And all ye need to know.

—Keats

Shirleen sat beside the fire sorting through the rest of the clothes. As she picked up another dress that she had sewn for her daughter a few months ago, and that had been worn by Megan only a couple of days ago, she brought the pretty garment to her nose and smelled it. Shirleen had not yet had the chance to wash it before her world had been torn asunder.

Oh, where was her precious child?

Shirleen felt the sting of tears in her eyes as she held the dress close to her cheek. The aroma of her daughter as she had always smelled right after a bath was still on the clothes as Shirleen had hoped it would be.

The thought of not being able to protect her child tore at her very being. Her heart ached as if someone were squeezing it.

As soon as she was able, she would leave

this place and go to the nearest fort to report her missing daughter.

She was certain the colonel in charge would send out the cavalry to search for Megan.

Shirleen would ride with them, for although she was not skilled at outdoorsy things since she had been such a homebody while growing up, she did know how to ride a horse. She had enjoyed an occasional outing with her father, horseback riding through the park on cool summer days.

At this moment she missed her papa almost as much as Megan, for he was the man who had always given her the courage to attempt things she otherwise could not face. He had always managed to make her wrongs right.

If he were there now to encourage her, surely the pain of missing her daughter would be more bearable. He would hold her close and tell her not to doubt that she would be reunited with her daughter.

"Oh, Papa, I do hope that I am reunited with Megan, and soon," she whispered to herself as she continued to hold the dress to her face, even though her tears were wetting it.

Lost in thought, Shirleen wasn't aware that she was no longer alone. She hadn't heard Speckled Fawn step quietly into the tepee.

She didn't realize that the woman had seen her hugging Megan's dress and crying. She didn't notice when Speckled Fawn silently withdrew.

Sighing, she placed the dress with Megan's

other clothes and then stacked her own things in a pile.

Having these things made her feel a little less lonesome for the happy life she had once known before she had been abused by her husband, for most of these clothes had been brought from Boston.

If not for the birth of her daughter, she would wish that she had never left Boston to journey to this dangerous territory with a man she too soon learned to fear. But she had heard so much about the exciting West that the opportunity to go there had been too tempting to let herself think about the possible pitfalls of living there.

Having chosen the clothes she would keep, she shoved the other things into the travel bag and took them to the entrance flap.

After shoving aside the skin hide, she set the clothes on the ground on the opposite side of the entranceway from where the warrior stood. He did not look down at her, did not seem even to know that she had leaned out from the tepee, if only for a moment.

She took the time to observe the activity of the village and caught sight of Speckled Fawn disappearing inside Chief Blue Thunder's large tepee.

Seeing the woman going there caused a spurt of surprising jealousy to rush through her. She did not like the idea that the white woman could come and go with such ease from this handsome Indian's lodge, as though she was something special to him.

Shirleen had to remind herself that this woman had a husband. Surely Blue Thunder was only her chief, a strange thought since she was white.

Shaking jealousy from her mind, and reminding herself it was foolish to fantasize over Blue Thunder, she turned and hurried back inside the tepee.

Because her meal had been interrupted earlier, she was still hungry, so she ladled another bowl of food out for herself.

As she slowly ate it, Shirleen could not stop herself from wondering why the other white woman had been going inside the chief's lodge.

"Speckled Fawn," Shirleen whispered between bites. "I wonder what her true name is, and why she chooses to go by an Indian name."

Yes, she was puzzled by everything about this woman. What in her past did she want to deny so badly that she had taken on an entirely new identity?

Chapter Eleven

I will be the gladdest thing under the sun,
I will touch a hundred flowers and not pick one.
I will look at cliffs and clouds
With quiet eyes.

—Millay

The early morning sun had just risen on a new day when Blue Thunder heard someone outside his lodge, waiting to be admitted.

When he opened the entrance flap, he discovered it was his uncle's wife, Speckled Fawn.

"Enter," Blue Thunder said as he gestured his visitor toward a thick pallet of furs near the lodge fire.

Speckled Fawn smiled weakly at him as she came further into the tepee, then sat down where she could look across the slowly burning flames in his firepit and see him clearly.

"Why have you come?" Blue Thunder asked, folding his arms across his muscled chest. "Is it about my uncle? Has he worsened since I last looked in on him?"

"He is no better, nor worse," Speckled Fawn said, nervously fidgeting with some fringe on her white doeskin dress.

"Then why have you come and interrupted my morning if not with news of my uncle?" Blue Thunder asked, though he had already guessed why.

He had seen her come and go from the white woman's lodge more than once.

Surely Speckled Fawn had appointed herself the woman's guardian since they both had the same color of skin.

But that was the only physical similarity between them. One was tiny and fragile-looking, the other full-bodied.

He had never had any true reason to dislike the one with the golden hair, especially since she had made his uncle so happy during his last days on this earth.

It was just that he had never wanted her among his people in the first place, to attract other unwanted whites there.

But thus far she had not been the cause of any misfortune to his village, instead she had brought good, since she had found a way to make an old man feel young again before he had become lost in his silent world.

Blue Thunder could not fault Speckled Fawn, for anything; she had fit in well enough with his people. He no longer worried about her being in the village.

"You do not speak yet as to why you are here, taking up the important time of your chief," Blue Thunder said, placing his hands on his knees as he crossed his legs at his ankles.

"Speak up, woman. You must have a reason for being here. Tell me what it is."

"Last night I visited the white woman," Speckled Fawn said softly. "I brought her some of the clothes taken by the renegades. When she saw them, she reacted strongly to the sight of a child's dress. I believe that dress belonged to her own child, a girl of perhaps four winters according to the size of the clothes. My chief, I saw the woman clinging to the dress and crying. I wonder where the child is, since she was not among those you rescued."

Blue Thunder's eyes narrowed as he continued to gaze at Speckled Fawn. "Do you really believe this woman is the mother of a small girl child?" he asked.

"Truly I do," Speckled Fawn murmured. "And although I introduced myself to her, and even asked her name, she did not offer it to me."

"Her name is Shirleen," Blue Thunder said, in his mind's eye seeing the beautiful, petite woman clinging to a tiny child's dress. He was touched to know that she might be a mother.

But that had to mean she also had a husband.

Perhaps he had been away from home when the massacre had occurred.

Knowing that the woman surely had both a child and a husband aroused jealousy in Blue Thunder's heart that he did not want to feel.

Although Shirleen had spoken to his heart with her lovely sweetness and vulnerabilty, it would be better if he could deny his attraction

to her. Her presence among his Wind Band
might draw unwelcome white people to his village. Among them could be a husband,
brother, or father, or even the cavalry searching for those who had been taken from their
homes by the renegades.

Ho, all of this could happen, and it would be
bad for his people. When white and red men's
lives collided, only trouble came from it.

But the possibility that this woman had a
child who had been stolen from her touched
his heart. He, too, had a daughter whom he
loved dearly. How could he ignore a parent's
sadness over the loss of a daughter?

"Blue Thunder, if Shirleen has been separated from her child, does this change your feelings about her?" Speckled Fawn dared to ask.

"The child might be with her *ahte*, her father," Blue Thunder suggested, even though he
did not truly believe she was. Why would an
ahte take a child to the trading post and not
ask his *mitawin*, his wife, to accompany him?

No, it did not seem logical.

"I doubt that," Speckled Fawn said. "A man
has no time to coddle a daughter while hunting,
or bargaining at a trading post. And surely the
woman's husband was hunting or getting supplies when the ambush happened at his home."

Seeing the logic in what she said, Blue
Thunder nodded.

"Blue Thunder, please send out warriors to
search for the child," Speckled Fawn begged.

She had always tried not to antagonize Blue

Thunder in any way, wanting to keep peace between herself and this powerful young chief.

But now things were different. If she needed to press her point about searching for the missing child, then so be it.

"Blue Thunder, if the child wandered away on her own, and is now all alone out there somewhere, it isn't fair to leave her at the mercy of two- or four-legged creatures that might happen along and find her," Speckled Fawn said, this time more forcefully.

She knew the chief had a kind, caring heart, especially where children were concerned. He had a daughter of his own and would never allow any harm to come to her. So she was sure she had reached him and that he would not ignore her pleadings.

"Speckled Fawn, leave me now," Blue Thunder said tightly.

"What are you going to do?" she blurted out, not caring that he might grow angry at her insistence.

"Speckled Fawn, you have said what you came to say," Blue Thunder replied. He rose to his feet and gently took her by the elbow to help her to her feet. "Go. I have listened. You are free now to sit with your husband."

Speckled Fawn walked with him to the entrance flap, allowing him to usher her from his lodge. She knew that she had been heard, and for her that was enough.

Now it was out of her hands. It was up to the chief to do what he knew was right.

Once outside, beneath a cloudy sky, Speckled Fawn turned and gave Blue Thunder a soft smile as he released his hold on her elbow.

"*Pila-maye*, thank you for listening," she murmured, then walked slowly away from him toward her own lodge, where she did plan to go and spend the rest of the morning with her husband.

Although she doubted he would hear much of what she said, she was still going to sit there and talk with him about the things he used to enjoy discussing after they first married.

He had been eager to know all about her, and she had told him the story of her life, everything except the bad, sad times that would never leave her. Those memories were imbedded in her heart, like leaves fossilized into stone.

But her life now was one of sweetness and peace. It was a vastly different world from the one she had known before coming to these wonderful people.

Blue Thunder watched Speckled Fawn until she disappeared inside her tepee. Then he turned slowly and gazed at the lodge where the other white woman temporarily made her home.

He had experienced many emotions since he had come face-to-face with the scarlet-haired woman. He had to deal with those feelings in the right way.

But now that he knew of a child who was surely in harm's way, the little girl must take precedence over everything and everyone else.

Chapter Twelve

Give me a mind that is not bound
That does not whimper, whine or sigh.

—Webb

Blue Thunder knew that he must not act too quickly on his decision to help Shirleen's little lost girl, or his people might see into his heart and feel that he was putting too much effort into this white woman's plight. She should just be another white woman to him, like Speckled Fawn. He should not be showing so much interest in her and her family.

He knew it was best not to think too much about this beautiful, flame-haired woman, but he could not help himself. She had touched his heart almost from the moment he'd seen her as he surveyed the Comanche renegades below him from the hilltop.

Her courage had called out to him. Captured by a fierce, murdering enemy, she had nonetheless walked boldly, proudly onward, as though to say to her captors that they had not gotten the best of her, and that she would survive whatever they did to her.

Ho, he had seen pride and courage in her, while all along she might have been mourning the loss of a child, not knowing whether she was dead or alive!

She was braver than most women he had known in his life, white or red-skinned.

His wife had been a woman of such strength, too. She had been dealt many hurts in her lifetime, but had never succumbed to them.

When he married her, he had taken her away from a spiteful sister whose jealousy had caused his wife much pain.

He had been so glad to separate Shawnta from that sister. He had actually married her more to protect her from hurts than out of love. Their marriage had been one of gentle understanding, full of quiet affection, but never passionate in any way.

He doubted the white woman would ever let any other woman, even a sister, stand in her way, or ridicule her.

Ho, she was tiny in build, but large in strength and courage!

And he knew that the more he allowed her into his mind, the more she was taking over his heart. Here was a woman who could take the place of the one he had lost.

He would always love Shawnta and the special way they had cared for one another.

But now he wanted a woman with whom he could share passion, not just affection. He wanted, oh, so much more than what he had had with Shawnta.

He wanted everything that he had denied himself while living in a marriage that was truly more of convenience than true, deep love.

He needed the enduring love that came with sharing his blankets with a woman who could inspire passion in him as well.

And if that woman's skin was white, so be it. His people would just have to accept his choice.

Suddenly aware of where he had allowed his thoughts to wander, Blue Thunder shook his head to clear his thoughts, stood quickly, and began pacing. He had thought too long about this white woman, who might still have a husband searching for her.

Although he must not allow himself to think about the woman again in such a way, the fact still remained that she might have a lost daughter. If a small child the same age as his own daughter was missing, it would be cruel not to search for her.

He gazed toward his closed entrance flap. He wondered if he should go and ask Shirleen about her daughter, yet thus far she had ignored him when he tried to talk to her.

She must hate all men with red skin. And why wouldn't she? It was Indians who had destroyed her world.

He hoped in time she would realize that not all people with red skin were bad!

If he could find her child, would that not convince her to trust him?

And although he did believe she had a husband out there somewhere, and although he knew he should fight his feelings for her, he could not help wanting to know more about her. She had spoken to his heart.

When he looked past the mistrust in her eyes, he saw someone who could be very loving and caring. First, though, he must gain her trust.

What better way to gain that trust than to find her daughter?

His decision made, he leaped to his feet, went to his entranceway and threw the skin door aside.

With determined steps he went from lodge to lodge, announcing a council with all of his warriors.

Soon they had gathered in the council house, their eyes questioning Blue Thunder as the morning sun filtered through the smoke that rose from the central fire. The men seated themselves around it, while their chief stood before them.

"My friends, it has come to my attention that the white woman who has been brought into our midst may have a *micinski,* a small child around the same age as my own, and that little girl has been separated from her *ina,* her mother," Blue Thunder said. "And why do I believe this might be so?"

He explained what Speckled Fawn had observed, and her belief that the woman who had escaped rape and death at the hands of the renegades had somehow become separated from her daughter.

His jaw tightened.

"The child might even now be with Big Nose," he said thickly. "I would not want to even think what his plans might be for the girl, for he is evil, through and through."

Black Wing, the troublemaker of the village, suddenly stood and placed his fists on his hips as he glared at his chief. "We should not get any more involved in the lives of white people than we already are," he growled out. "We already have two white women in our village. That is two too many. I say rid our lives of those two instead of bringing another one into our midst."

Blue Thunder gave Black Wing a scolding stare, causing the warrior to wince and quickly sit down again.

Blue Thunder then gazed slowly around him, making eye contact with each of his warriors before speaking again.

In their eyes was the trust that was lacking in Black Wing, and Blue Thunder knew they were always ready to do his bidding, no matter whom it concerned, or whether that person's skin was red or white. They trusted their chief in every way, and admired him deeply.

"It is my decision to search for this white child, who is probably around four winters of age. It is wrong for a child of this age, or any age, to be unprotected from men such as Big Nose and his renegades," Blue Thunder said.

"Those of you who will ride with me on a mission of kindness, stand. Those who wish to stay behind in the village for any reason, leave the council house."

The only one who left was Black Wing, and he did it with his head down and shoulders bent, looking like a coward.

Disappointed that even one of his warriors would oppose him, Blue Thunder felt betrayed by Black Wing. He would not forget this day.

He said nothing until Black Wing was gone. Then he looked at the warriors standing before him, dutiful as always.

"Here is my plan," he said firmly. "Separate yourselves into four groups. One group will stay behind to protect our village. You in the other three groups, leave the council house and mount your horses. Each group will ride from the village, then separate and travel in three directions. Search. You will look for two different things. One will be a child wandering alone, possibly even hurt, the other is Big Nose's hideout. If none of you are successful in finding the lost child, or Big Nose's hideout, return home at sunset."

He motioned toward the entrance flap with a hand. "Go," he said. "Mount your steeds. I will follow and mount my own. Once we have left the village, I will choose which group I shall ride with. But we must use all our skills today to find the child."

He stood aside as his warriors left in a flurry, then went outside himself.

He strode to his tepee and chose two weapons to take with him. One was a knife sheathed at his waist, the other a rifle.

When he left his lodge, a young brave was there with his saddled horse. He patted the boy lovingly on the head, slid his rifle into the gun boot at the right side of his white steed, then mounted and started to ride off with his waiting warriors.

But the feeling that eyes were on him made him pause for a moment.

He turned and found Shirleen peeking from the corner of the entrance flap of her assigned lodge.

Their eyes momentarily met, and then she dropped the flap closed.

Not certain why she was looking at him, wondering if he should take the time to tell her what he was doing, he paused a moment longer.

Remembering that she still had little reason to trust him or anyone in his village, he felt it was best not to tell her anything at this time. He hoped that when he returned he would have something positive to tell her.

If he could find her little girl, how happy she would be. It would be touching to see the two reunited.

Realizing that his warriors were beginning to wonder why he was lingering there so long, Blue Thunder looked straight ahead again, flicked his reins, and rode off with his men through the village.

He was determined to find the child.

After separating into three search parties, Blue Thunder rode straight and tall in his saddle at the head of one of them, his loose, thick, black hair blowing in the wind behind him.

His eyes did not miss any movement in the grass, or behind trees, or on the hillsides they rode past.

This search was as important as any task ever undertaken by himself and his warriors.

If there was a child, somehow, some way, he would find her!

Chapter Thirteen

Be strong!
Say not: The days are evil,
Who's to blame?

—Babcock

The day had been long.

The search had taken the Assiniboine war-riors far and wide.

But they were home now, empty-handed.

Blue Thunder had eaten the evening meal with his daughter and aunt. Bathed and dressed in fresh, fringed buckskins and match-ing moccasins, he stepped up to the entrance flap of the lodge where the white woman named Shirleen was staying. He imagined she must be feeling downcast, missing her old life with every fiber of her being, especially her daughter.

After spending a full day searching for the child, Blue Thunder spoke Shirleen's name before entering the lodge. He knew that she deserved as much privacy as anyone else, es-pecially since she was in unfamiliar surround-ings, at the mercy of people she did not yet trust.

Shirleen heard Blue Thunder's voice. It made her heart do a strange leap inside her chest. She realized she felt no fear at the sound of his deep, masculine voice.

Although she did not want him to know that she had any feelings for him, she could not help feeling more and more intrigued by the man. Would he think her attraction foolish, because she was a mere white woman and he was a powerful chief?

When the young chief spoke her name again, Shirleen hurried to her feet and went to the entrance flap.

Dismayed that her hand trembled as she reached for the hide covering, she seemed to have no control over her emotions.

As she held the flap aside, the evening breeze wafted past Blue Thunder into the small tepee, and she noticed the darkening sky behind him. Shirleen did not seem to know how to talk with him, fearing she might say the wrong thing.

She only looked at him shyly as he stepped past her, not waiting for her to invite him in.

As Shirleen dropped the skin back into place and returned to the fire to sit down beside it, Blue Thunder could not help feeling disappointed. He was discouraged that the woman still chose not to speak to him.

He sat down across the fire from her, noticing the hesitancy in her expression when her eyes momentarily met his.

When she looked away from him again, fixing

her gaze on the mats upon which she sat, Blue Thunder was overwhelmed by frustration.

"I have been gone most of the day with my warriors," he suddenly blurted out. "I am going to tell you where we have been, and what we did not achieve."

He waited for her to respond, but again she chose not to.

His frustration was building, for he truly wanted to help this woman.

But he also wanted her to want his help!

"I was brought news that you might have a child," he began.

Shirleen's throat tightened.

She looked quickly up at him.

But she still said nothing even though she was very aware that he was gazing into her eyes. She was also aware of how her own heart was racing.

She could not help wondering why he had concerned himself with news of her child.

He was a chief with many more things on his mind than the existence of a stranger's daughter.

"Is there a daughter?" Blue Thunder prodded.

When Shirleen still said nothing, he searched with his eyes for the small dress that Speckled Fawn had spoken of.

When he saw a tiny dress lying apart from the other clothes, he assumed it was the one Speckled Fawn had seen Shirleen crying over.

He moved to his feet and took the dress up into his hands.

She gasped when he suddenly turned and knelt on his haunches beside her, shoving the dress into her hand.

"This surely belongs to your daughter," he said. "You made the dress, did you not? Your daughter wore it."

Shirleen stifled a sob behind one hand as she held the dress in the other, her eyes filling with tears as she gazed directly into Blue Thunder's.

"You have been wrong not to tell me about your daughter," Blue Thunder said, standing and going back to sit across the fire from her. "There is a daughter, is there not?"

Shirleen fought against the emotions ravaging her heart as she started to say something, but it took too long, and he was speaking again.

"Speckled Fawn came to me and told me about your reaction to the tiny dress," Blue Thunder said thickly. "My warriors and I have searched the long day through for any signs of a small white girl child, but we did not find her."

Shirleen was too stunned to speak. She could not believe that this powerful chief would have made such an effort to search for a mere child, and a white one at that.

Why would a small child be so important to this Indian chief, unless he and his people needed white children for a particular purpose?

She suddenly went pale when a horrifying thought struck fear into her heart.

Did these people use white children as sacrifices to their gods?

The thought sickened her.

She stood quickly, dropped the dress to the mats, then ran past Blue Thunder. She stopped just outside the tepee and vomited.

The sentry's eyes widened as his chief came out of the tepee and hurried to the woman. He gently wiped her mouth clean with his own hand when Shirleen stopped vomiting.

Shirleen was stunned.

She turned her eyes up to Blue Thunder and stared disbelievingly at him as he wiped his hand clean on the grass, then stood and looked at her.

"Why did you react in such a way when all I wanted was to help you?" he asked, searching her green eyes for answers. "My people are not like the Comanche renegades who kill whites without a reason. I have no good feelings for whites, but I respect all people, as I do the animals of the forest. All were placed on earth for a purpose. A woman's purpose, whether red or white, is to bear and love children . . . and to give love to a man who will return her love in kind."

He dared to place a gentle hand on her cheek and gaze more intently into her eyes. "I see you as a lovely woman who has been wronged," he said thickly. "Is there a small child out there somewhere who has also been wronged?"

The touch of his hand was warm on her

cheek, the look in his eyes filled with caring. Shirleen felt anything but repulsed by him and what he was saying.

Now she felt foolish for having reacted so violently to what he had said.

She knew now just how wrong she was ever to think something so vile about him . . . or his people. He . . . they . . . had been nothing but giving and caring to her. And she had been nothing but cold and unresponsive in return.

That was not the sort of person she was, and she felt suddenly ashamed of herself.

If this man truly wanted to help her find her daughter, oh, how wonderful it was . . . how wonderful *he* was!

She was so taken by him and his kindness, she stepped away from him, leaned her face into her hands and sobbed hard.

"Come," Blue Thunder said softly. He gently took her by the elbow and walked with her back inside the tepee. He led her down on the pelts beside the fire, then picked up the tiny dress.

"Do you want to tell me now what this small dress means to you?" he asked, kneeling beside her.

Her eyes slowly lifted. "Yes, it means a lot to me," she murmured, a sob catching in the depths of her throat. "I did make this dress. It was sewn specifically for my daughter." She lowered her eyes and wiped tears from them. "I am so afraid that she . . . is . . . dead."

"Did the Comanche renegades take her?"

Blue Thunder asked as he gently placed the dress on Shirleen's lap. He felt keenly relieved that he had finally reached her heart, and that she was talking with him. "Was she taken by a renegade with a huge nose . . . the renegade leader who goes by the name Big Nose?"

"After I was abducted, I saw the man for a short while, and then . . . and then . . . he disappeared from the others," Shirleen said. "But no. As far as I know, he did not take my daughter."

She brushed fresh tears from her face and gazed into the midnight-dark eyes of the man who was quickly taking over her heart and making it his!

"When I looked outside, just before the attack, I saw that the gate to my yard was open," she said. "I also noticed that my daughter was no longer in the yard. She . . . she . . . might have wandered off on her own before the Indians came."

"My warriors and I will leave again tomorrow to search for your daughter," Blue Thunder said. He searched her eyes as she openly gazed into his. "Would you like to join the search? Can you ride a horse? Are you well enough, and strong enough, to accompany us?"

He believed that a woman, even wounded, would go to the ends of the earth to save her child.

He knew this to be true about Shirleen, for she had done nothing but mourn her loss since her arrival at his village!

He knew deep love when he saw it, and he saw it in this woman for her child.

Shirleen could hardly believe that Blue Thunder was actually offering her the opportunity to ride with him, to help search for Megan.

She was not at all sure what to say. Although everything within her cried out to do as he suggested, she was afraid to say yes.

His world was vastly different from hers.

And there was the question of trust again.

Although everything inside her heart told her that this man was trustworthy to the very core of his being, he was still an Indian, and she had seen the atrocities other Indians had committed.

Filled with conflicting emotions, she lowered her head and did not respond to his question. She actually was too breathless to speak.

Trying to understand her stubbornness, her continued obvious distrust of him, Blue Thunder stared at her for a moment longer, then left quickly.

Shirleen realized now just what she had done by not speaking up right away. She should have agreed to his kind offer, even if it had seemed out of place for such a strong chief as he to include a woman, a tiny white woman at that, in his plans.

Thinking that she had surely insulted him, and thinking she had lost her chance to do as he had suggested, Shirleen threw herself down on the blankets beside the fire and cried.

Chapter Fourteen

There are loyal hearts,
There are spirits brave,
There are souls that are
  Pure and true.

—Bridges

Shirleen looked quickly up and wiped her eyes with the back of a hand when she heard some-one enter her tepee. She stared in disbelief when she saw who was there. It was Blue Thunder with a little girl who appeared about the same age as Megan. And like Megan, this little Indian girl was beautiful, her copper skin so soft-looking, so smooth.

The child did not seem to have any fear of this white stranger. She stood calmly beside Blue Thunder, holding a doll that seemed to be made from corn husks, with a tiny piece of what looked like fox fur wrapped and tied around it.

Oh, how sweet and precious the child looked in her tiny, beaded doeskin dress.

Her tiny feet were encased in knee-high moccasins that seemed from the same fabric as her dress.

Her long black hair hung loosely down her little back, held in place by a thin, beaded headband.

Her eyes were the blackest of black, and large. She stared back at Shirleen with a searching look, yet her expression was friendly enough.

Blue Thunder suddenly gave the little girl a gentle shove toward Shirleen. Shirleen slowly stood up, wondering why the child had been brought here.

The little girl stopped after taking one step. She stood there quietly, gazing up into Shirleen's eyes, the doll still hanging in one hand at her side.

"I, too, have a daughter," Blue Thunder said, stepping up beside the child. "I have brought her here to introduce you to her. She is called by the name Little Bee. Does she not seem to be the same age as your daughter? I believe the dress made for the white child would fit my daughter were she to put it on."

Shirleen was stunned speechless that Blue Thunder had a daughter. No one had mentioned that fact to her, but why would they? They would think that his having a daughter should mean nothing to her, so why make mention of her?

But it did mean something to Shirleen.

It meant that although Blue Thunder had lost his wife, he still had someone he loved deeply.

A child.

Oh, yes, a child could mend many a broken heart.

If she had not had Megan, Shirleen would never have survived the life she'd known with Earl, a man who had beaten her just for the fun of it.

Yes, a child could make life worth living. If Shirleen could have her own daughter with her, things could be somewhat normal again.

Blue Thunder sank to his haunches facing his daughter. "Do you remember what we talked about before coming to this lodge?" he murmured, lovingly stroking his fingers through her long, thick hair.

Little Bee nodded anxiously as she looked into her father's eyes.

"Then take the doll to the woman," Blue Thunder softly urged. "Her name is Shirleen. Remember how I told you that she has a daughter?"

Little Bee nodded again, smiling.

"You told me that this doll will be for her little girl when she is found and brought to our village," Little Bee said softly. "I have more than one doll. It is good to share with someone else."

"That is right," Blue Thunder said, patting Little Bee on her soft cheek. "The doll you give the lost child will make her happy again when she is found. When you get to know each other, you can play with your dolls together."

Little Bee smiled widely as she stepped around her father and went to Shirleen.

Blue Thunder stood up and watched as his daughter held the doll out before her.

"Please take this and give it to your daughter after she is brought to our village," Little Bee said. "It will be fun playing dolls with her."

Deeply touched, Shirleen took the doll and held it to her bosom.

"Thank you," she said. "It is a beautiful doll. You are sweet to part with it."

"What is your daughter's name?" Little Bee asked, searching Shirleen's green eyes, mystified by their color.

Shirleen felt suddenly ashamed that it had taken her so long to make up her mind about Blue Thunder.

Now she knew that all he had done had been undertaken out of kindness.

Even more than that.

She had seen interest in his eyes. She believed that he was having feelings about her much like her own about him.

She felt as though she had finally found a man whose every thought and move showed a deep sense of caring, not only for his people, but also . . . for her!

She felt so ashamed that she had mistrusted him, but knew she must move past her embarrassment.

She felt as though she had been given a reprieve, a new beginning, a second chance, with Blue Thunder.

Shirleen cradled the tiny doll in her left arm, while with her right hand she gently touched

Little Bee's face. "My daughter's name is Megan," she said, her voice breaking at the very mention of her child. "She is four years old, and as beautiful and giving as you." She swallowed hard. "You will be the best of friends."

Blue Thunder felt keen relief wash through him. Finally, the barrier between himself and Shirleen had been broken, and all because of the sweetness of a small child.

Yes, children were the future, and his daughter's generous behaviour today was proof of that!

Her innocence, her sincerity, were all that was needed to win Shirleen's trust.

He stepped closer to Shirleen. Placing a hand on his daughter's little shoulder, he smiled at Shirleen. "Can you not see how sincere I am in wanting to help you find your daughter?" he asked gently. "Tomorrow another search will be made for her. If you feel strong enough, you can go with me and my warriors."

Before Shirleen had a chance to answer, a woman came into the tepee and carried Little Bee out with her.

"That is my aunt," Blue Thunder said. "She is called Bright Sun. She is a widow. Since my wife's death, my aunt cares for Little Bee. They have a strong bond between them. It is a good thing, this love my aunt gives my daughter. At first, when Little Bee realized that her mother would never hold or love her again, she cried for many sleeps. But once she got past the initial shock of loss and sadness, she accepted my aunt as a substitute mother."

"I'm so glad," Shirleen said, having seen the love in his aunt's eyes as she had swept Little Bee into her arms and carried her from the tepee. "The loss of a parent can be horrible, especially a mother."

"You have not said anything about your husband," Blue Thunder said, settling down on some of the rich pelts beside Shirleen as she seated herself near the fire.

Shirleen stiffened at first. The question made her uncomfortable, because she had hidden the ugliness of her husband's treatment of her from everyone she knew.

But now?

Yes, she felt that it was time to tell someone about this horrible man, or tell at least enough to let Blue Thunder know that she no longer considered Earl as her husband.

She was beginning a new life without him, and she was not going to worry that she had not been given a legal divorce.

To her, Earl was no longer her husband, even if it was written on paper that he still was.

In her heart she was now totally free of this man.

She would never look back and wonder whether she had done the right thing by planning to take Megan from her father.

He was not a fit husband, or father!

"Yes, I have a husband, yet I no longer consider myself a wife," Shirleen said. "If the Comanche renegades had not come, I would have fled the heartless, cruel man. As it is, the end result is the same. He . . . is . . . no longer a part of my life, nor my daughter Megan's."

When Blue Thunder saw that Shirleen had said all that she felt comfortable saying about her husband, he did not press the issue. She seemed uneasy and bitter at the very mention of the man, so he would not question her further about him now.

But in time he would know everything about her and the man she apparently loathed with every fiber of her being.

Now that he understood her circumstances, Blue Thunder was beginning to see the promise of many tomorrows with this woman. The more he learned about her, the more he cared for her.

No wonder she had evaded his questions and seemed uneasy in his presence. He knew now that her behavior was the result of how she had been treated by another man.

He could understand her hesitance to trust him. Her husband had apparently given her cause not to trust any man.

But Blue Thunder had finally broken down the barrier she had placed between them, and he was oh, so happy for it!

Yet . . . she *was* a woman who had fled her husband, and in the world of the Assiniboine, no woman left a husband once she had spoken vows with him. Loyalty ran deep among his people.

But neither were husbands cruel to their wives.

He wondered just how far the husband's cruelty had gone. In time he would learn, for he wanted to know everything about Shirleen.

"You have not yet given me an answer about tomorrow," he said, changing the subject, which seemed to have made Shirleen tense again. "Will you travel with me and my warriors as we set out again to search for your daughter? If you are with us, and we find a wandering child, you can identify her."

"Oh, I do wish to go with you," Shirleen quickly said. "I must admit to some continued pain in my head, but I am no longer as dizzy as I was. I believe I am well enough to ride my horse. Thank you for being so kind. You . . . are . . . truly generous."

"I do hope to bring you and your child together again," Blue Thunder said thickly. "No mother should be separated from her child. I hope to reunite you and your Megan."

He gazed into her eyes. "But you must be certain you are able to ride a horse, for once you are on it and we are far from my village, it will take some time to return," Blue Thunder said. "That journey back home could be grueling if you are in pain."

"Blue Thunder, the true pain is in my heart because I miss my daughter so much. I am so worried about her," Shirleen said, a sob catching in her throat. "I will suffer whatever pain I must, if it means I can help find her."

"She will be found," Blue Thunder said with a certainty that made Shirleen truly believe that soon she would be holding her daughter in her arms.

And if that were so, she would never let Megan out of her sight again.

Tomorrow couldn't come fast enough now for Shirleen!

Chapter Fifteen

Under the arch of life, I saw
Beauty enthroned, and
Tho her gaze struck awe,
I drew it in as simply as my breath.

—Rossetti

The morning sky was cloudy and Shirleen could feel moisture settling on her face as fog crept over the village while she brought her horse from the corral and readied it for travel.

When it was saddled, she looked from tepee to tepee, hoping to see one or more warriors leave their homes, prepared to accompany her and Blue Thunder on the search for her daughter.

But she was still the only one who had come outside. Clearly, she was the most anxious to begin the search for Megan.

Sighing, she clung to her horse's reins and shifted her feet nervously on the ground as she waited for the warriors to say good-bye to their wives and children. Even Blue Thunder must be spending some last moments with his daughter.

As for her, she had hardly slept, she was so eager to begin the search.

She had lain in her bed of blankets and pelts the entire night, clutching Megan's dress, as she impateitly awaited dawn's arrival.

When the soft light of morning finally filtered through the smoke that wafted up from what was left of her fire, she hadn't been able to get up fast enough to dress for the day's journey.

After untangling her hair with a brush she'd found among the clothes in the travel bag Speckled Fawn had brought to her, Shirleen had quickly pulled on her clothes.

Wanting to keep her fire burning while she was gone, because both the days and evenings were cool now, she had placed several logs on what remained of her lodge fire. There was plenty of wood in the stack of logs that had been brought for her daily use.

Her thoughts were interrupted as first one and then another warrior came from their tepees and took horses from their personal corrals.

Her heart thumped wildly in her chest, for the moment had finally arrived when she would be riding alongside the handsome chief and his warriors.

As she mounted her horse, her leather skirt hiked up past her knees, revealing the leather boots that were also among the things Speckled Fawn had brought for her to choose from.

It seemed strange how fate had returned to her these physical reminders of her normal life.

The fog had finally lifted, and the wind was cool against her face as Shirleen saw Blue Thunder walking toward her. He was leading a beautiful white horse.

She felt a strange tingling rush through her veins when Blue Thunder stopped beside her and mounted his horse, then turned a soft smile her way.

"Are you ready?" he asked as his warriors banded together in one tight group, awaiting his orders to ride. "Are you truly strong enough to travel?"

It was at this very moment, after having mounted her own horse, that Shirleen realized she was in no shape to ride. The lump on her head throbbed, and she suddenly felt dizziness rush through her. But she couldn't think of herself.

Her daughter's life lay in the balance!

Shirleen had to be strong enough to accompany these warriors to search for Megan.

"Yes, I am well enough to travel," Shirleen murmured, trying hard not to show that she was dizzy. She held her reins tightly as she smiled over at Blue Thunder. "Please. Let's go now. I hardly slept a wink last night, I was so eager for this moment to arrive."

"A . . . wink?" Blue Thunder said, arching an eyebrow. "What is this . . . wink?"

His curiosity about the unknown term made Shirleen's feelings for him deepen even more.

"It is a way to say that I had trouble sleeping," she said, smiling softly at him.

"You had problems because you did not feel well?" Blue Thunder asked, truly concerned about her welfare.

He noticed that she was weaving slightly as she sat in the saddle. He was quite certain that she was dizzy, even though she would not admit it.

And he understood why.

She wanted to be part of the search for her daughter.

The child meant the world to her, just as Little Bee did to Blue Thunder!

"No, that wasn't the reason," Shirleen said, telling the necessary white lie. "It was because of my anxiousness to go and search for my Megan. Each day I am away from her is one day too many."

"We shall do what we can to find her," Blue Thunder promised. "I understand the hurt in your heart. It would be the same way I would feel if my daughter were no longer safely with me."

"Thank you for your understanding," Shirleen murmured. She looked toward his aunt's tepee and saw the woman holding Little Bee in her arms. Both were gazing at Blue Thunder, awaiting the moment when he would ride away.

Seeing Little Bee made Shirleen's heart ache even more for her own daughter. She hoped that today that heartbreak would end.

Oh, if only God would make it so!

Her gaze shifted when she saw Speckled Fawn step out of her tepee.

Speckled Fawn waved at Shirleen, and it seemed to Shirleen that she was whispering "Good luck" to her.

Shirleen was now beginning to believe that the woman truly did want to be her friend. Needing one badly, she smiled and waved back at Speckled Fawn. Silently she mouthed "Thank you."

She looked straight ahead again and held the reins tightly, her knees locked against the sides of her horse in the hope that it would keep her steady when dizziness claimed her again. Slowly they made their way out of the village.

As they rode on and on, each pounding of her horse's hooves made Shirleen feel less able to keep up the pace. But determination was her company today.

It kept her going, no matter how dizzy she was at times.

Finally they reached their destination, the site of her former home, where her friends had died, and where their cabins and barns had been burned to the ground.

They didn't go all the way to the scene of the massacre, but close enough for Shirleen to see the dead lying upon the ground.

She felt a bitter bile rise into her throat and had to fight off the urge to vomit as she turned her eyes quickly away from the gruesome scene.

She wanted to ask Blue Thunder to please see to her friends' burials, but there was hardly anything left . . . to . . . bury. The roaming, hungry wild animals had had their way with the bodies.

Shirleen knew that she would have trouble even identifying anyone. Only their clothes gave a clue to each person's identity, but otherwise, there was no way to know who was who.

Feeling suddenly so beaten at the thought that her daughter might be somewhere in the same sort of shape, Shirleen hung her head and cried.

Blue Thunder saw her despair.

He could even feel it inside his own heart.

He sidled his horse closer to hers. "I am sorry for what you see here today, and for what you are experiencing inside your heart," he said, reaching over and gently touching her arm. "I believed the menfolk would have returned to bury these bodies. Otherwise I would not have brought you this close to where the massacre happened."

"We had to come here in order for you to track my daughter," Shirleen sobbed. "So please do not concern yourself over me. There is only one person now who must have our attention. Megan."

"I have prayed to Wakonda, who created all things, that your daughter will be put in our path today," Blue Thunder said. He eased his hand away from her. "If not today, tomorrow. I am as determined as you to see that you and your daughter are reunited."

He looked slowly in all directions. "That is

how it was meant to be," he said. "Daughters and mothers should never be separated from one another."

He gazed into her eyes again. "Unless it is death that causes such a separation, as it was for my daughter and her mother," he said. "My Little Bee lost her mother due to the same insanity that has separated you from your Megan. The same sort of men, those who wish only to murder and steal, are responsible for your loss and mine."

"I pray to God that I will be reunited with my daughter," Shirleen said, her voice catching.

"We will begin the search now," Blue Thunder said, reaching over and touching her cheek, letting his thumb caress her flesh.

Shirleen almost melted into her saddle at the feelings of rapture caused by Blue Thunder's flesh touching her own. She was thrilled by the way he was caressing her so lovingly.

She understood now that his willingness to search for her daughter was as much for Shirleen's sake as for Megan's.

She knew that Blue Thunder felt something special for her.

She felt foolish now for those moments when she had had doubts about him, especially when she had actually run from him and vomited when her imagination had run so out of control!

"I don't think I will ever be able to repay you for your kindness toward me," Shirleen murmured as he took his hand away and took up his reins with both hands.

"No payment is needed," Blue Thunder said.

He looked at his warriors, who were waiting for his instructions, and who had been a witness to his feelings for Shirleen.

He knew that they had seen him gently touching and stroking the white woman's face, and how softly he had spoken to her.

So be it, for there was no denying to anyone how he felt about Shirleen. Fortunately, now that she had let her guard down and was allowing herself to see things as they really were, she was beginning to care for him, too.

"My warriors, spread out in all directions and begin to search in this area, close to where Shirleen's cabin once stood," Blue Thunder instructed, looking from one man to the other. "There are many footprints, but all you will look for are small ones. The child is the same age as my Little Bee, so you should be able to judge the size of the tracks. Also, search everywhere a small child might hide. Look behind every bush, tree, boulder, and even search for a cave. If she was not captured, but instead wandered off, she might have gone anywhere; she may have hidden to wait until her mother came for her."

That possibility brought more sobs from the depths of Shirleen's throat, for she knew that her daughter could be at this very moment wondering where her mother was.

Today's emphasis was to be on searching this area. If her daughter wasn't found, then the hunt for the renegades' hideout would continue tomorrow.

Shirleen rode alongside Blue Thunder, searching the woods as he looked closely everywhere that he thought a child might try to hide.

She remembered how, as a child, she had played hide and seek with friends in Boston. She knew the art of hiding well, because of those innocent games. She tried to imagine where her daughter might have gone to hide.

But even after hours of searching, no signs of Megan were found.

As the sun crept lower in the sky, Blue Thunder looked over at Shirleen and saw how bone-tired she was. Though the night would soon spread its dark cloak over the land, he decided it was best that they not take the long ride back to the village just yet.

She needed to rest, and then later, if she seemed strong enough, they would make the journey back to his home.

But if not, they would sleep beneath the stars.

He reached over and gently took her reins, stopping her steed as he brought his own to a halt. "It is time to return home, but I do not think it is in your best interest to accompany the others," he said. "You need to rest, and then we will resume our journey once I see you are able."

Shirleen was unutterably sad that they had

not found Megan, and her body was one big ache. Feeling exhausted from riding so long, she nodded. "Yes, I think what you have decided is best," she murmured. "I truly don't think I could go much farther."

"Then we will stay here and let my warriors go," Blue Thunder said.

He rode away from her and went to explain their next course of action to his warriors.

Some gave him a strange sort of questioning look, while others nodded and accepted that whatever their chief decided was right for all concerned.

Blue Thunder watched them ride away, then returned to Shirleen, who was already out of her saddle and leaning against a tree, her eyes half closed.

Blue Thunder dismounted and went to her. "I will tether our steeds," he said. "I see a place that will be good for us to make camp and rest."

The realization that he had said they would make camp, which surely meant he was readying a campsite for a full night instead of only a little while, made Shirleen's heart skip a beat.

She looked at him, studying his expression as he secured the horses, and hoped that her trust in him was warranted. She had never been alone with an Indian before, except for those moments when Blue Thunder had sat with her in her tepee.

But this was different.

They were completely alone.

And she knew that he had feelings for her.

There was no hiding his feelings now. They were evident in the way he looked at her; the gentleness with which he treated her. Both attested to the fact that he had fallen in love with her. And she now knew she felt the same for him.

She just could not believe that a man such as he would force himself on any woman.

Being so tired, and knowing she had no other choice but to do as he asked tonight, she went willingly with him to make camp beside a meandering stream.

She was glad that the moon was out tonight in all its glory. The countryside was lit up almost as bright as day.

She sat down on blankets that Blue Thunder had spread out for her, then watched him prepare a fire.

When the flames were sending off soft light all around them and the smoke was spiraling into the sky, Blue Thunder came and knelt down before Shirleen.

"I will be away for a short time," he said softly.

"Where are you going?" Shirleen asked, her eyes widening in fear.

"I am going to scare a couple of rabbits from their burrow," he said. He smiled softly at her. "We will have a nice meal. Then we will rest beside the fire. When you are ready to ride again, all you have to do is tell me."

Again seeing how foolish she had been to

doubt him for even one moment, Shirleen smiled and nodded. Then she stretched out on the blanket while he departed for his brief hunt.

He came back a short time later, carrying two skinned animals. Shirleen had not heard the sound of a gunshot, and she sat up and questioned him with her eyes.

"A knife makes a quiet, quick kill," he said, already placing one of the animals on a spit that he prepared over the fire, and then securing the second one beside it.

Shirleen saw that this was a good time to go and wash the day's dirt off her face and hands before they settled beside the fire to eat. She was looking forward to some nourishing meat.

Blue Thunder watched her go to the stream. He didn't accompany her, for he felt that she needed privacy to attend to her needs.

When she momentarily slipped behind some bushes, he knew that she would relieve herself of one of her discomforts.

As she came from behind the bushes and looked his way, she was blushing so pink he could even see it beneath the light of the moon. He had not anticipated this timid side of her that she was revealing to him.

He smiled and nodded and watched as she knelt beside the stream and washed her face, and then dipped her hair into the water and washed it.

When she stood, with the moon glowing on her wet hair and face, it was hard for Blue

Thunder to just sit there looking at her, when everything within him wanted to go and draw her into his arms and kiss her.

All of those thoughts were quickly erased when Shirleen suddenly screamed and grabbed at her head. As she collapsed to the ground, moaning and holding her face in her hands, Blue Thunder could not get to her quickly enough.

When he reached her, he swept her up into his arms and carried her to the blankets, where he gently laid her down.

He knelt beside her as she gazed up at him through tears.

"My head," she sobbed, reaching for it. "A sudden, sharp, searing pain shot through the wound on my head."

"Is it still hurting?" Blue Thunder asked as he swept her hair back from her face.

"It has subsided somewhat," Shirleen said, her voice catching as she slowly sat up. "Thank you again for being so kind and caring."

"Who would not be kind and caring toward you?" Blue Thunder said thickly as he gently wrapped a blanket around her shoulders.

Never in her life had Shirleen met a man as gentle as Blue Thunder.

Not even her papa had been this gentle.

Blue Thunder's kindness, caring, and gentleness melted Shirleen's heart.

She knew now that she was lost, heart and soul, to this man.

The color of his skin didn't matter.

Yet there was still that question she had not yet asked him.

"Why did you have me guarded when you brought me to your village?" she blurted out.

"Why?" Blue Thunder repeated, reaching over and testing the doneness of the meat. It still had a ways to go before being ready to eat.

He drew his hand back and looked over at Shirleen, slowly smiling. "You thought that you were being held captive?" he asked, searching her eyes.

"How could I think otherwise?" she asked.

"I had you guarded from others who might sneak into my village under the cover of darkness and try to steal you away," Blue Thunder softly explained. "The guard was not there to prevent you from leaving, for you have never been a captive. You were brought to my village so my shaman could make you well, and for nothing else."

"I am so glad to know that you never saw me as a captive," Shirleen murmured. "I . . ."

When she started to say something but then fell silent, Blue Thunder's curiosity was piqued. "What more do you want to say?" he asked, again searching her eyes and finding them so beautiful.

Even beneath the moonlight they shone so mystically green.

"I . . . I . . . shouldn't," Shirleen said, blushing.

She had came close to saying that she thought perhaps he had brought her to the village because he was enamored of her, just as she was of him.

But she knew this was not the time to reveal such a thing to him.

She wanted to be certain of his feelings first.

"Then don't," Blue Thunder said, his pulse racing. He had hoped she was about to reveal her feelings for him.

"It is time to eat," Blue Thunder said quickly. "The meat is dripping its juices into the flames. I prefer them to be in my mouth, do you not, too?"

"Yes, I truly do," Shirleen said, laughing softly. Strange how her head no longer ached, how her seat was no longer sore from long hours in the saddle.

She suddenly felt as though she might be floating above herself. She was now absolutely certain that she was in love with a man who also loved her.

And she would not let the fact that she was married mar the beautiful relationship that was developing between herself and this handsome, wonderful man.

In her eyes, she truly was no longer married to the cruel, heartless man she had grown to detest . . . even hate.

In the West, life could be abruptly snuffed out at any time, so she was going to take advantage of each and every moment that she had breath left in her lungs.

She blushed as Blue Thunder handed her a piece of hot meat.

"Be careful, it might burn your fingers," Blue Thunder said, wanting to protect her from even such a tiny annoyance as that.

"I will," she said, smiling softly at him. She was happy for the first time in so long, but her full happiness would not come until she held her daughter in her arms again!

When she took her first bite of the meat, she gave Blue Thunder a quick, puzzled look. "I have eaten rabbit often," she said. "This tastes nothing like rabbit. It has the taste of . . . chicken."

He chuckled. "I did not come across rabbits but instead sage hens," he said. "That is why you taste sage hen, not rabbit."

"Well, my word," Shirleen said, laughing as she gazed down at the piece of meat held between her fingers. "I have heard of sage hens, but have never eaten one."

"Do you prefer sage hens or rabbit?" he asked, pulling off a big bite of meat for himself.

"Sage hens," she said. "It reminds me of the turkeys my mother cooked on Thanksgiving."

"I will catch you a wild turkey one of these days," Blue Thunder said, smiling as he enjoyed relaxed, inconsequential talk with this woman . . . a woman he now knew that he would love forever.

"I would enjoy that," she murmured.

Thinking about a future that had Blue Thunder in it made her feel suddenly at peace with herself, except for one thing—not having Megan with her.

But she believed that this handsome chief would eventually find her daughter, for was there anything he could not do?

She smiled timidly at him as she took another bite of meat.

He returned the smile, awakening new feelings in Shirleen that she never knew existed!

Chapter Sixteen

Our lives would grow together
In sad or singing weather . . .
If love were what the rose is,
And I were like the leaf.

—Swinburne

The sound of people talking somewhere not far
away awakened Shirleen with a start.

She leaned up on an elbow and found Blue
Thunder sitting beside her where she lay on
comfortable pelts beside a slow-burning lodge
fire.

The voices she had heard came from outside
the tepee, a tepee she suddenly realized was
not the one where she had been staying.

And why had Blue Thunder been sitting beside her as she slept?

And . . . how had she gotten there?

The last thing she recalled was falling asleep
beside the campfire where they had stopped to
rest before returning to the Assiniboine village.

Whose tepee was this? she wondered.

As she looked slowly around her, she saw
that the buffalo-hide walls had been painted
with scenes of the exploits of the person who

lived there. She also saw quite a cache of weapons stored at the back of the tepee.

"I am very confused," Shirleen said as she sat up, realizing that she wore the clothes she had worn on her journey to search for Megan.

She gazed into Blue Thunder's eyes as the blanket that had covered her fell away. "How did I get here?" she softly questioned. "The last I remember is becoming so sleepy I could not keep my eyes open."

"You fell asleep," Blue Thunder said, gently pushing a fallen lock of her hair back from her puzzled eyes. "I did not think it wise to spend the full night away from my home with the renegades about. They are always a threat, often roaming the darkness in search of horses to steal, so I rode back to my village with you."

"But . . . if I was asleep . . ." Shirleen said softly. "Blue Thunder, I still don't recall anything past sitting by the campfire. I surely would remember riding on my horse."

"You did not ride on your steed," Blue Thunder said, bringing even more confusion into Shirleen's eyes. "I led your horse while you rode on mine with me."

"But . . . why don't I even remember that?" she asked, getting more confused by the minute. "What are you not telling me?"

"I carried you on my horse while you lay in my arms, asleep," Blue Thunder said, smiling softly at her.

Utterly stunned by what he had just revealed, that she had been held in this wonderfully handsome warrior's arms while she slept, Shirleen was rendered speechless.

Seeing that she was perplexed by what he had told her, Blue Thunder reached over and gently touched her cheek. "You are in my personal lodge," he said. "As you can see, it is much larger and has more comforts than the one that was assigned to you. While you slept I brought your clothes from the other tepee, as well as those of your daughter."

Shirleen found it hard to think while he held his hand on her cheek, his dark eyes gazing into hers.

He had to know just how mesmerized she was by him.

But the fact that she was now going to be staying in his lodge made her feel suddenly apprehensive.

Had he brought her there out of kindness, or lust? Did he believe that she was totally his now, to do with as he pleased?

She wanted so badly to trust his motives, to believe he was helping her out of kindness. Now that she would be in such close proximity to him, she would surely discover the truth very soon.

Whatever happened, she would be eternally grateful that Blue Thunder had rescued her, that she was not wandering alone, or a captive of the renegade Comanche.

She was also very happy that she had not come to this village as a captive.

One thing was certain: She could not feel any

more enamored of a man than she was of Blue Thunder.

She prayed that his intentions toward her were as pure and honorable as they seemed to be. Most of all, she prayed he would be able to find Megan.

The fact that her daughter was still nowhere to be found made everything else in her life seem empty and worthless. Feelings for a man, her own welfare, came second to her daughter, and there was not one thing that she, personally, could do to find Megan!

"I will be leaving soon with my warriors to make another search for your daughter today," Blue Thunder said, as though he had read her thoughts.

In reality, he had read the emotion in her eyes. They changed, it seemed, by the minute.

He knew that her worry for her daughter was uppermost in her mind now. He hoped to remedy that.

"I just can't thank you enough for your kindness," Shirleen said, her voice breaking. "My daughter Megan means the world to me. Without her, I feel a strange sort of cold death inside me."

"I hope to take away that terrible feeling," he said, taking his hand from her cheek. "I hope to fill your heart with sheer joy when I hand your daughter Megan over to you."

"It *would* be a joyous moment," Shirleen said, smiling at him. "Again, thank you."

"When I leave, there is someone who would

like to talk with you," Blue Thunder said, rising to his feet.

"Who?" Shirleen asked, glancing past him at the closed entrance flap.

"Speckled Fawn," Blue Thunder said, walking to the doorway. He stopped and gave her a questioning look. "Can I tell her that you have said it is alright for her to come in for a while?"

"Yes, please do," Shirleen said.

She rose from the pelts, and had at least gotten her hair straightened with her fingers when the white woman arrived. Shirleen smiled at Speckled Fawn, who came in and actually gently embraced her. As she stepped away, there was true sympathy in her eyes.

"I am so sorry that you didn't find your daughter," Speckled Fawn said. "If I had a child out there alone, I would feel the same heartbreak as you. As it is, I never had a child, and it now seems that I never shall. My husband is elderly, and I would not even think to marry again once he is gone. He is the only decent man to have held me in his arms. There surely is no other."

Shirleen could think of one man whose arms were so comfortable and sweet.

Blue Thunder's.

She only hoped that, in time, more than sadness would bring them together.

She would love for him to hold her and say sweet things to her that would make her melt in his arms.

She even dared to daydream of him actually kissing her.

"I'm glad that you found happiness with your husband," Shirleen murmured, gesturing with a hand for Speckled Fawn to sit beside the fire.

After Speckled Fawn seated herself, Shirleen settled down onto the pelts next to her.

"Food will be brought soon," Speckled Fawn said. She drew her knees up before her, hugging them. "Would you rather I stay or leave?"

"Please stay," Shirleen said. "And I apologize for the times that I have been rude. I have been so distraught. And . . . I wasn't sure whether or not to trust anyone, or whether I was safe in this village."

"And now?" Speckled Fawn asked, searching Shirleen's eyes.

"I feel so many things," Shirleen admitted.

She lowered her eyes timidly when she thought of how she felt about Blue Thunder.

Oh, surely her love would show on her face if she even mentioned his name!

"I hope that now you realize among those feelings is the realization that I am a friend," Speckled Fawn said, seeing that Shirleen was still having trouble speaking her mind fully. "And I hope you realize that all of the people in this village are your friends, especially Blue Thunder and our shaman, Morning Thunder."

"I do believe that now," Shirleen said, looking up at Speckled Fawn. "But you should understand why I was so hesitant. It was hard to

trust any Indian after suffering so much at the
hands of those . . . other . . . Indians."

"Many whites call all Indians savages. Those
who speak so loosely about things they do not
truly know are people whom one should avoid.
They are wrong to label such an innocent people as the Assiniboine savage," Speckled Fawn
said angrily, her protective feelings for her
adopted people obvious. "There are true savages among those whose skin is red, the sort
who spread fear as they roam the land killing,
scalping, and raping."

"You and I are the lucky ones," Shirleen
murmured, slowly nodding. "If Blue Thunder
and his warriors had not arrived when they did
that day, I imagine I would either be dead now,
or wish that I was. I would never want to live if
I were raped, or if I knew that those renegades
took my daughter's life."

"I am certain that Blue Thunder will find
your daughter," Speckled Fawn said reassuringly as she reached over and patted Shirleen
on the arm. "He is a determined man when he
cares deeply about something, or someone. It
is obvious that he cares for you, and also for
your daughter, since she is your child."

"I so hope that he can somehow find Megan
and bring her to me," Shirleen said, swallowing hard.

Hoping to change the subject, for the very
mention of Megan broke her heart, Shirleen
smiled at Speckled Fawn and forced herself to
act interested in someone else.

"You have told me a little about how you came to be with these people," Shirleen said. "Would you mind telling me more?"

"I think it would be good for me to talk about it," Speckled Fawn said. She swallowed hard, then gazed into Shirleen's green eyes. "It all began when my parents chose to move from civilization as I had always known it. Back East there were no Indians, nor men who would take advantage of a girl in, oh, so many wrongful ways."

Shirleen listened intently to Speckled Fawn's story, stunned by the tale of this white woman who'd lost her family on her way to Wyoming and had been left to fend for herself after she escaped a gang of highwaymen.

Speckled Fawn grew teary-eyed as she reached the worst part of her story. She had been forced to fend for herself as she had fled from one town to another, dancing in saloons and dance halls for her survival, from age eighteen to when she was thirty. She had no other skills she could use to make a living.

It had been then, in the unruly town of Iron Gulch, Wyoming, that a drunken man forced her into a room and attempted to rape her. The only way she could stop him was to kill him with his own knife.

She fled that town, and heard later that wanted posters had been put up about her. Fortunately, the drawing was not truly her likeness, so no one had found her.

Speckled Fawn had wandered and wandered, on river boats, across land on foot, on stolen horses, with no one caring about her. One day she collapsed between towns from sheer exhaustion and hunger.

She woke up in this Assinboine village, bathed, dressed in a lovely doeskin tunic and moccasins, with her hair in one long braid down her back. Then an even stranger thing had happened.

An elderly Indian came to the tepee where she had been placed. He had stood there just slowly looking her over.

After gazing silently at her for a short while, he had left.

A while later, Chief Blue Thunder came and told her that she had been chosen to marry his elderly uncle, who had been their shaman before he grew too tired and old to do his duty any longer.

Stunned, Speckled Fawn had asked why the uncle would want her.

Blue Thunder had told her that his uncle's mind had begun to leave him. Because he loved the elderly man so much, Blue Thunder did everything possible to make his uncle happy while he still could.

Speckled Fawn had listened, astonished, when Blue Thunder explained that his uncle had said he wanted the white woman to be his wife.

Blue Thunder had assumed from this request that his uncle's mind was worse than he had thought it was. His illness must be robbing his mind of reason, for why else would he want a white wife, especially one who was many moons younger than he?

No, Blue Thunder had never understood why, but to make his uncle content during these last moons of his life, he had asked Speckled Fawn, whose true name was Kathleen, if she would humor his uncle by marrying him.

Feeling as though that might be the answer to all of her woes, Speckled Fawn had not hesitated to agree to this special request of a man who was loved and admired by so many. She would be kept safe under the wing of these people who loved the old man.

"And so there it is, the story of how I happened to be married to a much older man, an Indian who was once a powerful shaman," Speckled Fawn said. "We have never consummated our marriage. He just seemed happy to have me as his wife, especially when we were in our blankets. He never fondled me in any way. He was just content that I was there, smelling good like a woman smells, and warming his blankets for him."

"The story has such sweetness about it," Shirleen murmured. "I admire you so much for finding the good in your marriage. Do you miss that . . . part of marriage that can bring joy into a woman's heart, if you are with the right man? You know what I mean."

Shirleen had always wondered how it would be to make love with a man she loved, not be

forced into a sexual confrontation with someone she detested.

"No, I never even thought about such
things," Speckled Fawn said softly. "I had had
such a horrible life after my parents died. I
wanted nothing more to do with men. I saw
this life that was offered me as something you
would read in a fairy tale. I have been oh, so
very, very happy here, except when I realized
that my husband's mind had finished its journey of slipping away. Now when he looks at me,
I'm not sure if he truly sees me. But his smile.
Ah, his smile has always warmed my heart,
even now, when I am not certain if he is aware
of smiling at me."

"And even after he no longer knew you, these
people allowed you to stay as his wife?"
Shirleen murmured.

"Yes, I was allowed to stay in the capacity of
his wife, because the Assiniboine people knew
that my presence continues to bring Dancing
Shadow peace even though he has lost his
ability to speak, or perhaps even . . . to think
rationally," Speckled Fawn said.

Tears filled her eyes. "But, oh, how he can
smile," she murmured. "I love his smile. It
brightens a room. And oh, how I do love . . .
and . . . adore him."

She paused, then said, "It was my husband
who gave me the name Speckled Fawn because
of the freckles on my face."

"It is such a pretty name," Shirleen said,
sighing. "Did I tell you that Morning Thunder

gave me an Indian name? Tiny Flames. Is it not ever so beautiful?"

"Yes, it is pretty. I assume the color of your hair and your petiteness prompted the name," Speckled Fawn said, smiling. "I do love it, Shirleen. Would you rather I call you by your Indian name?"

"For now, my given name is probably better," Shirleen said. "Perhaps later, the other. It all has to do with how things turn out."

"I sense that you have feelings for Blue Thunder that are very, very special," Speckled Fawn said, searching Shirleen's eyes. "You do, don't you?"

"How could I not?" Shirleen admitted. "I have never met anyone like him before. He is such a kind, generous, and caring man. And . . . so . . . loving."

"I have seen how he looks at you and treats you," Speckled Fawn said. "I have not seen that look in his eyes since before his wife died. But there seems to be more sparkle in his eyes as he looks at you than when his wife was still with him."

"Oh, surely you are wrong," Shirleen said, stunned that Speckled Fawn would be so open with her.

"I don't think so," Speckled Fawn said, then looked more seriously at Shirleen. "I have told you my story. Are you ready to tell me yours? I know about your child, but not your husband. There was a husband, wasn't there?"

"There was, there is, but I no longer claim

him as such," Shirleen said tightly. "On the day of the massacre, when the renegades came and changed my life forever and robbed me of my beloved daughter, I . . . I . . . was packed and ready to leave my husband. He had gone to the trading post, and I was taking the opportunity to flee while I could. I was just putting the last things in my bags when I heard the first war cry from the renegades."

She glanced over her shoulder at the travel bag, then looked at Speckled Fawn again. "Most of those clothes you brought me were the ones I had packed," she murmured "They were stolen by the renegades."

"You were actually leaving your husband?" Speckled Fawn gasped, her eyes widening. "Why?"

Shirleen lowered her eyes, swallowed hard, then stood up and turned her back to Speckled Fawn.

Shirleen turned and slowly lowered the bodice of her doeskin dress, leaving her scarred back exposed to Speckled Fawn's stunned eyes.

"My Lord," Speckled Fawn gasped, aghast at what she saw. "Did that man, your husband, do that to you?"

"Many, many times," Shirleen said, bringing her bodice back into place.

She turned toward Speckled Fawn again and slowly sat down. "It didn't take much for my husband to decide to remove his belt and use it on me," she said miserably. "He truly didn't need a reason for doing it. He seemed to take joy from seeing me react to the beatings. My main regret, even more than the pain I went through, was that my daughter saw her papa do this to me. The sight is surely engraved on her tiny heart and brain forever and ever."

"Lordie, lordie," was all that Speckled Fawn could say.

"I was so afraid that one of those beatings might kill me, and so afraid of what this was doing to my daughter, I decided to leave with Megan," Shirleen said, tears filling her eyes. "But my plan was foiled by the Comanche renegades."

Shirleen realized that for the first time since she had met this kind woman, Speckled Fawn was rendered speechless.

Chapter Seventeen

She is most fair, and thereunto,
Her life doth rightly harmonize.

—Lowell

Always missing his daughter when he was separated from her, Blue Thunder was with Little Bee at his Aunt Bright Sun's lodge. Bright Sun was down at the river, getting fresh water.

Ever so lovingly, Blue Thunder was holding Little Bee on his lap beside the slow-burning lodge fire while she was proudly showing him a new doll made by a friend's mother.

Blue Thunder smiled at all the questions that came from his daughter's mouth today; he enjoyed her inquisitive side. When she was a grown woman, her curiosity would cause her to question many things before allowing a man into her life as her husband.

"Who is the white lady who is new to our village?" Little Bee asked, gazing intently into her father's midnight-dark eyes. "Why is she still here in our village? Is she going to marry our shaman like the other white woman married Dancing Shadow?"

"No, the woman is not going to marry Morning Thunder," Blue Thunder said, his eyes gleaming with pride and love for this wonderful child of his. "And who is she? I am only finding out myself who she truly is and what her life was before I saved her from the renegades."

He paused, then said, "And where did she come from? She had her own family before she was stolen away by the renegades."

That last statement, that last truth, was hard for Blue Thunder to say. If this woman had no husband, he would have already kissed her and held her to his heart as he asked her to be his wife.

But as it was, he had much to sort through before they could act on their feelings for one another.

He would never forget that she had told him she was ready to leave her husband before the renegades had arrived and changed her life forever. He wondered what the man had done to make her want to turn her back on him.

He understood how much courage it must have taken to actually plan to set out from home, alone with her child.

He hoped to get all the answers soon, for he wanted to make Shirleen part of his life.

Ho, he was going to marry her.

He would find a way to help her straighten

out her life, for she deserved far more than what life had brought her until now.

"*Ahte*, I know that you have searched for the woman's little girl more than once. Have you finally found her?" Little Bee asked, her eyes wide as she thought about the doll she had given to the mother for that other little girl.

"No, she has not been found," Blue Thunder said thickly, feeling a pang of regret that he could not give his daughter a more positive answer.

He drew Little Bee gently into his arms. "Little Bee, my *micinski*, I am so proud of you," he said as she dropped her doll so that she could fling her arms around his neck, returning his loving embrace. "I know I have told you more than once that I am in awe of you. You are only four winters of age, yet you have the intelligence of someone much, much older."

"That is because my *ahte* is *gauche*, chief," Little Bee said proudly. She leaned a little away from him so that she could give him a wide smile as she gazed into his eyes.

Blue Thunder laughed softly as he returned her loving gaze.

A voice speaking his name from beyond the entrance flap drew Blue Thunder's attention from this special moment with his daughter. He regretted that it had been brought to an end all too soon.

He recognized the voice.

It was Two Moons, one of his most favored warriors.

"Little Bee, I must go and see what brings Two Moons in search of me," Blue Thunder said, gently placing her on her feet.

He bent low and kissed her cheek. "Play with your new doll while I am gone," he encouraged as he stepped away from her. "She needs a big hug, do you not think so?"

Little Bee giggled and nodded her head, then hurriedly picked the doll up and gave it a hug.

Blue Thunder stepped outside. "Two Moons, what brings you to my aunt's lodge?" he asked, concerned when he saw his warrior's serious expression.

"One of our scouts has come to have council with you, my chief," Two Moons said. "He says that he might have news of the child. He is waiting for you in the council house."

Blue Thunder's pulse raced at the thought of possibly hearing something that might lead him to Shirleen's daughter.

He would enjoy seeing Shirleen's reaction when he put the child into her loving arms.

"*Pila-maye*, thank you, Two Moons," Blue Thunder said, walking away from him. He could not arrive quickly enough at the council house, where the scout awaited his arrival.

When he stepped inside, he hurried over to where his scout Proud Horse stood beside the lodge fire. Proud Horse turned quickly to receive Blue Thunder's manly embrace.

Blue Thunder stepped away from Proud

Horse and gestured with a hand toward the pelts beside the fire. "Sit," he said, sitting down himself as Proud Horse made himself comfortable. "Now tell me what news you have brought to me about the child."

"My chief, when I was at Fort Dennison this morning, questioning the people there, I saw a white man with his daughter, who is four winters of age, the same age the white woman said her daughter was," he explained. "He was bragging about how he had duped his wife by stealing the child from her. He said that he was now waiting for the next riverboat so that he could take his daughter far away from her mother. That riverboat should arrive after one more sunrise."

"Was the name of the child spoken?" Blue Thunder asked, trying to hold down his eagerness to leave and see if the child truly was Shirleen's daughter. If so, he would not return to this village without her!

"*Ho*, the *ahte* spoke the name Megan to his white friends," Proud Horse said, drawing a quiet gasp and then a broad smile from Blue Thunder.

He knew now that everything was going to happen as he had prayed it would.

He would rescue the *micinski*.

He would then pursue a way to make Shirleen his *mitawin*, his wife!

He would not allow the husband to stand in the way of his need for this woman. He wanted her so badly, his heart ached for her to be in his arms, their lips touching tenderly as they shared that first, wondrous kiss.

Ho, he would find a way, for when he wanted something as much as he wanted this woman, nothing would stand in his way!

Up until now he had been a patient man.

Well, his patience had just left him!

Chapter Eighteen

Oh! Who would inhabit
This black world alone?

—Moore

Knowing just how anxious Shirleen was about her daughter's welfare, Blue Thunder hurried from the council house to his tepee. He stopped just outside the entrance flap.

He suddenly realized that Shirleen might not be completely happy about his news. Yes, she would be jubilant that her *micinski* was alive, and not held by the murderous renegades.

But she could also be filled with dread that Megan might not be rescued soon enough and her husband could get on the riverboat and disappear with Megan for the rest of her life.

Shirleen would also surely be filled with more hate for her husband than she felt already. It would be awful to learn that he had been planning to abduct his daughter for some time, just waiting for the right opportunity, and had finally found it.

Surely he had somehow discovered Shirleen's

plan to leave him and to take his daughter away from him.

From all that Blue Thunder now knew about the man, he had not abducted Megan out of love for her, but out of spite for the woman who was her mother. He had taken the child to retaliate against Shirleen's plan to leave him.

Blue Thunder urged Proud Horse to finish his story quickly. He wanted to leave soon for the fort, to rescue the child before the man could board the riverboat.

From what Proud Horse told him, there was still time to get to the fort, because the riverboat was not expected to arrive until after one more sunrise.

Blue Thunder knew the spot where the riverboat landed, because he had been curious about this large canoe that traveled from place to place. He had gone more than once to watch it from a hidden place, where no whites would see him.

The riverboat had what were called "paddlewheels." He'd been fascinated by how they turned constantly in the river, water dripping from them, churning and splashing into the huge wake that was left behind by the boat.

He had studied the people aboard the boats. He had seen that most were white pony soldiers, because he recognized their attire.

He had often also seen women and children with white men who wore no soldier attire. He knew that these were more settlers coming to this land that had once belonged solely to the red man.

At that time, Blue Thunder had resented them all.

But now?

He had found one white-skinned person that he would never resent, only love.

He looked over his shoulder at his warriors, who were already in their personal corrals behind their tepees, readying themselves for the journey to Fort Dennison.

Having waited long enough, perhaps even too long, since he knew Shirleen would want the news quickly, he brushed the entrance flap aside.

He stepped inside his lodge and found Speckled Fawn there talking to Shirleen.

Realizing that Speckled Fawn cared for Shirleen, he decided to include her in what he was about to reveal to the woman he now loved with every beat of his heart.

Soon he would reveal his feelings to Shirleen, just as soon as the child was rescued and brought to her mother.

He would not think otherwise.

Both Shirleen and Speckled Fawn looked up at Blue Thunder at the same moment. He continued to stand in the entrance, without coming farther into the lodge.

Shirleen's heart skipped a beat, for she saw something in Blue Thunder's expression that told her he had come there with news, and . . . surely it was news of her daughter.

As somber as he was, her heart now sank. Oh, surely, dear Lord, the news *was* about her beloved Megan and surely it was not good!

She rushed to her feet and went to stand directly before Blue Thunder.

She looked pleadingly into his eyes, yet she was now truly afraid to hear what he had to say.

If it was bad news about her daughter, if he was going to tell her that Megan was dead, she would want to die, too!

Seeing how distraught his silence was making Shirleen, realizing that he should not have hesitated before telling her the news, Blue Thunder gripped her softly by her shoulders and returned her steady gaze.

He did not smile, for he was not sure how Shirleen would receive the news.

She would be most definitely torn between conflicting feelings.

"News has been brought to me about a child," Blue Thunder said, stiffening when Shirleen gasped and went suddenly pale.

"She is alive," he rushed out, knowing that was the most important part of this news he had brought her.

He realized he had gone about telling her in the wrong way. He should have told her that Megan was alive the moment he stepped into the lodge.

But now he had to tell her the rest of it, and as he did this, he watched her eyes take on a different hue. And her cheeks suddenly bloomed with a flush that was surely caused by anger toward her husband.

"How could he have done this?" Shirleen cried as she gazed into Blue Thunder's dark eyes. "Why didn't I see signs that he was planning to take Megan away?"

She hung her head. "Oh, dear Lord," she said in a much lower tone. "Oh, surely he found the bags and supplies beneath the bed. He knew from that what I had planned, and beat me to it. He took Megan away before I could leave, myself, with her. He was never even planning to go to the fort to trade!"

A sudden hot rage filled her very being.

She stepped away from Blue Thunder so that his hands were no longer on her shoulders. She had been keenly aware of the warmth of his hands, which had penetrated the doeskin fabric of her dress right into her flesh.

She had loved that tingling warmth, reveling in the gentleness of his hands. But now she had something very different on her mind. She had to find a way to rescue her daughter from a father whose heart was cold toward Shirleen, and who might have taken revenge for what she had been planning to do by stealing her precious child!

She doubled her hands into tight fists at her sides. "The fiend," she said, her voice catching. "He doesn't love Megan enough to care for her as she should be cared for! How dare he! No . . . child . . . should be without her mother!"

Speckled Fawn rose to her feet and went to Shirleen. She placed a gentle hand on her arm and turned Shirleen to face her. "No matter why he did this, Shirleen, we must waste no more time talking about it," she said, her eyes filled with hatred for a man who could be so cruel to a sweet woman like Shirleen.

Beating a defenseless woman was a crime that God would never forgive!

And then there was the child.

Oh, surely she was scared to death being away from her mother, especially after having witnessed her papa beat her mother so often. Megan surely expected to be beaten, herself, whenever the man had a mind to do it.

Speckled Fawn looked more intently into Shirleen's eyes. "Dear, you know that your daughter is with a demon," she said. "Show Blue Thunder what he did to you. Your back, Shirleen. Turn and show him . . . your back."

Her emotions were so raw that tears stung her eyes as Shirleen gazed at Speckled Fawn. Then she turned slowly to Blue Thunder, whose eyes were filled with questions about what Speckled Fawn had just asked Shirleen to do.

Remembering how gentle Blue Thunder had been to her from the very moment of her rescue, Shirleen turned her back to him and slowly lowered the bodice of her doeskin dress, so that the scars on her back were revealed to him.

She did not even feel awkward at exposing so much of her body to this man, for soon she hoped to be with him fully unclothed. She longed to discover what true lovemaking was all about.

Always when Earl had gone to bed with her, she had clenched her teeth and trembled until he was done with her. She had grown to hate those nightly duties.

But now she looked forward to the time when she would discover the wonders of joining her body with a man.

With Blue Thunder.

Shirleen heard Blue Thunder gasp and knew that he was horrified by what he saw, as horrified as she always was to know that she was scarred like that for life.

Blue Thunder could hardly hold his rage when he saw what that heartless man had done to this woman, a woman who was so tiny, so fragile and defenseless. She could never have fought back, or she would have died trying.

His heart ached for Shirleen. Now he knew something else he must do besides finding her daughter. He would punish the white man who had dared to raise a hand to her. Blue Thunder reached out for Shirleen, gently pulled her dress back up on her shoulders, then turned her to face him.

He framed her beautiful face between his hands as he gazed into eyes the color of grass. "My woman, my woman," he said thickly. "I

will go for your daughter. I will bring her home
to you."

Then with overflowing emotion, he brought
Shirleen into his gentle, loving embrace.

Shirleen felt a warmth, a passion, rush
through her that she had never before felt. She
was elated to hear him call her his woman, and
to know that he was going to bring Megan
"home." Already he saw Megan and Shirleen as
a part of his life.

And then there was the way he was lovingly
holding her in his arms.

She leaned her cheek against his powerful,
bare chest, inhaling the smell of him that was
now so familiar to her.

It was a mixture of clean, sweet, river water
and the outdoors, the kind of wondrous aroma
that she had scented on a beautiful spring
morning in Boston.

For a moment, she was lost in his embrace.
She was not even thinking of the cruelties of
life, but only how happy she was that this
wonderful man cared about her, and in turn,
her daughter!

If he did succeed in bringing Megan back to
her, oh, what a wonderful father he would be to
her daughter. She knew that she was going to
marry this man, even though by law she was
still married to a demon.

She knew that God was a good, understanding God, and he would understand that she
must break the vows she had spoken with
Earl, a man she'd truly never known.

After that first beating, she had learned the truth, that he was the sort of man who saw women as nothing more than punching bags.

She believed that God would bless her union with this man, Blue Thunder, who truly did seem to cherish her.

So, too, would he cherish her daughter, for who could not? Megan was the sweetest, loveliest child on the earth!

But thinking of Megan again and where she now was, Shirleen's eyes filled with tears.

She leaned away from Blue Thunder and gazed into his midnight-dark eyes. "How?" she asked, a sob catching in her throat. "How can you rescue my daughter? Earl is at the fort, surrounded by the cavalry, who will never allow you to take a white child from her white father. And if you did have a plan of rescue that you feel might work, could you even get there in time?"

Suddenly Speckled Fawn spoke up, after being unusually quiet for so long. "How well does your husband hold his liquor?" she asked, stepping up to Shirleen as Shirleen slipped from Blue Thunder's arms and turned to face her.

Shirleen was stunned by the question, wondering what on earth that had to do with anything.

"Shirleen, how well does your husband hold his liquor?" Speckled Fawn repeated, more insistently.

"Hardly at all," Shirleen replied. "You see,

while I was with Earl, there was scarcely enough money for food and supplies, much less for liquor. But when Earl did manage to get some whiskey, he drank it all at once. He got drunk fast." She lowered her eyes. "That was when I got my worst beatings," she said, her voice breaking.

"Speckled Fawn, why would you ask such a question?" Blue Thunder said, his voice tight with controlled anger. He did not like to see Shirleen so upset.

"I have a plan, if you will only listen," Speckled Fawn said, realizing that once again she had not only annoyed her chief, but also angered him. "Will you listen, my chief? I believe I know of a way to get the child from her father."

Blue Thunder sighed heavily, then nodded. "Tell us the plan," he said, this time not so impatiently. He had realized that Speckled Fawn was a woman of much intelligence. She had lived a hard life before coming to live among his people. She had gotten herself out of enough "scrapes," as she called them, to have a good sense of what might work now.

Yes, he was ready to listen to whatever plan the golden-haired white woman had come up with.

Shirleen listened, her eyes widening with every word Speckled Fawn said. She began to realize that this woman was very intelligent, and knew ways to outsmart men who were stronger than she but not as clever.

The more Speckled Fawn said, the more certain Shirleen felt that soon, finally, Earl would get his comeuppance.

But best of all, Shirleen began to believe that soon she would have her daughter back in her arms!

A disturbing thought occurred to her. Earl must have taken Megan from their yard only moments before the Indians had arrived with their war cries and eagerness to kill and rape.

Surely Earl had grabbed Megan and had hidden amid the thick forest of trees near their cabin just in time to see the Indians approaching. No doubt he had clasped his hand roughly over his daughter's mouth, first to keep her from crying out for her mother, and then to keep her from letting the Indians know where they were.

Now that she thought about it, she was certain that Earl had witnessed the murders, the rapes, the burning of the cabins and barns. He had even seen Shirleen lying there unconscious, then taken away with ropes tied around her waist, and had not done a thing about it.

When he had reached the fort, he probably had not even told the colonel in charge about the massacre, for had he done this, when Shirleen and Blue Thunder and his warriors returned to where the massacre had happened, the bodies would have been buried by the cavalry.

No, Earl had not told anyone what he had witnessed. He cared nothing for those who were left dead upon the ground. He had done nothing while women were raped right before his eyes.

She was sure this was true, because Earl most certainly had not had time to get very far away after taking Megan. The time span between the child's disappearance and the renegades' attack had been too short for him to have fled.

If he had tried, he and Megan would have been added to the casualties.

The one thing that puzzled her was why he had waited so long to steal Megan. He had been gone for many hours before actually taking the child from the yard.

Then the reason came to her. Until that moment, when Shirleen had allowed Megan to go outside alone, Megan had been safely in the house with her mother.

Allowing Megan to go outside had played right into Earl's hands. It had made Earl's plan work to perfection.

Shirleen had never hated Earl more than she did at this moment of realization.

Chapter Nineteen

A merry heart goes all the day,
A sad tires in a mile.

—Shakespeare

Shirleen found it hard to believe that Speckled Fawn was willing to place herself in danger to help her and her daughter Megan.

She still stared disbelievingly at the woman whom she had first mistrusted so much she would not even speak with her. Now she trusted Speckled Fawn implicitly. She had clear evidence of her kind and giving nature.

"No, I can't allow you to take such a chance," Shirleen suddenly blurted out. "What you are suggesting might not only get you killed, but also Megan."

Speckled Fawn put her hand gently on Shirleen's shoulder. "You want Megan back, don't you?" she asked, gazing intently into Shirleen's eyes.

"You know I do," Shirleen said, returning the gaze. "But what you suggest doing is so . . . dangerous. You might never be able to return to this village. It would be horrible if that happened. I would blame myself, always."

"Forget everything but your daughter's welfare," Speckled Fawn said. She took Shirleen by the hand and urged her to sit beside her, while Blue Thunder sat on Shirleen's other side. "We must give this plan a try. I won't have it any other way."

"Shirleen, do you understand the plan?" Blue Thunder asked, impressed by Speckled Fawn's eagerness to help.

He was beginning to see her in a different light and felt that he had been wrong to ignore her as he always had.

"Not altogether," Shirleen murmured.

"Then let us go over it again so that you do understand it," Blue Thunder said. "Speckled Fawn, myself, and my warriors will go to the fort under the pretense of needing to trade at the post there. We recently had a good hunt, so the pony soldiers will not think we are there for any other purpose than to trade. While we are making an actual trade, we will make sure that the man who is waiting for the riverboat with his child goes by the name Earl Mingus, and if the child's name is Megan. If so, we will set Speckled Fawn's plan in motion. She will go to the fort alone after my warriors and I leave. She will be dressed in the clothes of a white woman and will pretend to be a woman in distress."

He looked around Shirleen and nodded at

Speckled Fawn. "Speckled Fawn, you tell the rest, since you will be the one living it," he said.

Speckled Fawn nodded and began speaking in a low voice as she continued telling Shirleen the plan. "As Blue Thunder said, I will arrive at the fort as a woman in distress. I will say that I am the only survivor of a Comanche attack on my cabin. I will say that my husband and child are dead and that there are no bodies to retrieve. I will say that the renegades took the bodies with them to prevent anyone from the fort giving them a decent Christian burial. I will plead for safe asylum at Fort Dennison until the next riverboat arrives so that I can leave this godforsaken place forever."

She paused, then said, "I know the fort commander will take me in and care for me; he will pity me as a woman who has lost everything. After earning the soldiers' trust, I will ask for something that might raise a few eyebrows."

"Whiskey?" Shirleen asked, remembering part of the plan as Speckled Fawn had outlined it to Blue Thunder.

"Yes, whiskey," Speckled Fawn said, smiling almost wickedly.

"But, Speckled Fawn, surely most women don't go to the fort requesting whiskey," Shirleen said, her eyes filled with uncertainty.

"No, I'm sure they don't, but I am a woman, remember, who has lost everything," Speckled Fawn said. "They will think that having seen my family murdered might have caused me to lose some of my senses, making me ask for something that normally I would not ask for. But I expect them to give me anything I want because of how pitiful I will appear. I will explain that my reason for wanting the whiskey is to forget my woes . . . my losses. I will explain that I am not normally a drinking woman, but after what I have been through, I need something to numb my memories of how my family died so horribly. I will say that I need to drown the pain of my loss in whiskey."

Speckled Fawn paused, then continued, "I will find Earl then, and get on his good side by showing him the whiskey. I will tell him I'll share it with him if he wants some. Hopefully, he will agree, and will take me into his cabin with him. I'll make sure that he drinks much more than I, until he is as drunk as a skunk."

"But, Speckled Fawn," Shirleen said, interrupting her. "If you do manage to get in his cabin with him, might he not take advantage of you sexually?"

"Surely he wouldn't do that, not while his daughter is there," Speckled Fawn said. "Anyway, what I plan to do is ply him with whiskey until he's so drunk he won't know what hit him. Hopefully, he'll pass out from it. That's when I will have the chance to get Megan away from him. I will wait until it is dark so that the sentries at the fort won't be able to see my movements. I will then take Megan where Blue Thunder and his warriors will be waiting for me."

"I still see many loopholes in the plan," Shirleen said. "First, you told me you are a wanted woman whose likeness is on posters. Won't the men at the fort recognize you and see right through your plan and arrest you?"

"Those posters were placed here and there five long years ago," Speckled Fawn said. "My picture was only one little speck on the wall, surrounded by many of the worst criminals in the area. Surely by now the posters, which didn't even look like me, have been yanked down and thrown away, replaced by pictures of other, more hardened criminals. Also, I have gained a lot of weight since those posters were put up, and my hair was dyed red back then. I am a natural blonde now. And I am confident that I am more likely to succeed than fail."

"But, Speckled Fawn, when Earl sobers up and comes to realize what happened, when he finds Megan gone, all hell will break loose," Shirleen said, her voice tight. "A search party will surely be sent out to look for you and Megan. I can't see Earl just standing by and allowing a woman to get the best of him."

"By then I will be safe back in the village. The men at the fort won't have any reason to suspect that Indians had anything to do with this," Speckled Fawn said in a tone of confidence. "To them, I will have disappeared from the face of the earth with the child."

"I believe Speckled Fawn's plan can work," Blue Thunder said, drawing both women's eyes to him. "It doesn't matter how it is done, just as long as the child is brought safely back to her mother. Her father is evil, through and through. Our main focus here must be to get the child back to her mother."

He reached over and placed a gentle hand on Shirleen's cheek. "But it is up to you, whether or not you want to give this plan a try," he said softly.

"Why are you doing this for me?" Shirleen wondered aloud. "I am still . . . no more than a stranger to you. You . . . truly . . . don't know me."

He moved closer to her and reached his arms around her to draw her close. "I do know you," he said thickly. "I know your goodness. I know your sweetness. And I know that you are a devoted mother and how much you are missing your daughter."

He placed his hands on her shoulders and gazed directly into her eyes. "You have suffered too much already in your life, especially at the hands of the evil white man who calls himself your husband," he said tightly. "You have never deserved such inhumanity as that man showed you. You are a good woman."

He paused, then said as he lowered his hands from her shoulders, "My daughter no longer has a mother," he said softly. "I cannot allow yours to suffer in the same way as my daughter, never being able to see her mother again."

He framed her face between his hands. Their gazes met and held. "Don't you know, deep down inside yourself, that you are now way more than a stranger to me?" he said hoarsely. "You surely know how deeply I care for you."

The heat of a blush rushed to Shirleen's cheeks. "Yes, I know," she murmured. "Now I do know that you care for me. I . . . I . . . guess I have known for sometime now."

"Then trust that I will bring your child home to you, no matter what," Blue Thunder said. He wrapped his arms around her, drawing her into his gentle embrace.

She returned the hug, hating to let him go.

But she knew that this was not the time to think of herself and her need for Blue Thunder. It was time to focus fully on Megan. Only Megan.

She eased herself from Blue Thunder's arms and turned to Speckled Fawn. "Why are you risking so much for me? Until recently, I was only a stranger to you," she said.

"Yes, perhaps a stranger, but I now see us as soul mates," Speckled Fawn said, smiling into Shirleen's eyes. "And know this, soul mate. I will help bring your daughter home to you. At any cost, Shirleen. At any cost."

Shirleen reached over and embraced Speckled Fawn. "Please, oh, please, come home unharmed," she said, her voice catching. "I have never met a woman such as you, a woman who gives of herself so unselfishly."

"I only want to give back some of the kindness shown to me by the Wind Band," Speckled Fawn said, tears filling her eyes. "Things could have been so different for us both. We were so fortunate to have been found and taken in by these wonderful people. I want your daughter to be a part of this life, too."

"And she will be," Blue Thunder said firmly as he managed to hug both women at once. "She will."

Chapter Twenty

She was swayed in her suppleness to and fro,
By each gust of passion.
                                    —Des Prez

Just as Speckled Fawn left through the entranceway, dropping the flap closed behind her, Blue Thunder turned to Shirleen. "Soon I must leave, but I feel a need to leave you with something that will help you pass the time more peacefully," he said huskily.

He reached out and drew her into his embrace, all the while gazing down into her eyes. "I want to show you just how much I love you," he said. "Will . . . you . . . allow it? I want you to see how a man can make gentle love to a woman. I want to be that man. I want you to be that woman."

"I never wanted or needed my husband in a sexual way," Shirleen said, on fire inside with needs she had never felt before.

But she had never been in love before.

She had thought she might be in love with Earl, but after their first time together in bed, she had known the horrible mistake she had made by marrying him.

She had been left cold by his hands, his lips, his brusqueness. He had taken her virginity and had not allowed her to feel anything but pain, then dread.

He had taken his pleasure from her body, giving nothing back.

Each time after the first, it had been so quick. He had shoved himself into her a few times, and then as soon as he received his pleasure had rolled away from her, not interested in whether or not she had felt anything.

It had always been one-sided.

All that he had cared about was himself.

She had grown to hate seeing the sun set, knowing what would ensue. She had been so glad when her monthly period arrived, for that would give her some reprieve . . . until Earl had not even taken that into consideration and had forced himself on her anyhow.

The first time she begged him not to, he had used his razor strap on her.

"You seem lost in thought," Blue Thunder said. He placed a hand beneath her chin and lifted it so that they could look into each other's eyes. She had lowered them as she became lost in sordid memories.

"I'm so sorry," she said, near tears. "I . . . I . . . was wrong to allow my mind to wander at such a time as this, but there is such a difference between the way you treat me and the way I was treated by the man I married. And even though all of this has happened so quickly between you and me, I do love you so, Blue Thunder, and . . . I . . . do want you so badly."

"I will never harm you in any way," Blue Thunder said, brushing soft kisses across her brow. "My woman, oh, how I love you. I need you."

"I am yours," Shirleen said, smiling sweetly at him as the tears dried in her eyes. She was now only thinking of this wonderful man and the coming moments when she knew she would finally discover how wonderful love-making could be.

This man she loved with all her heart was so gentle, so caring, so loving!

She trembled with ecstasy as Blue Thunder slowly, almost meditatively, removed her clothes, bending to one knee to take off her moccasins, slowly, one at a time, while still gazing up into her eyes.

What he did then made Shirleen's heart skip a beat. She was uncertain whether it was right or wrong; all she knew was the sheer bliss it was causing inside her. He placed his hands at her hips and drew her closer to him, his tongue flicking out and touching, then caressing, that part of her which had only now come alive.

She threw her head back in ecstasy, moaning with a pleasure she had never known existed, as he continued to caress her there with his tongue.

And then she was aware that he was kissing

his way up her body, causing tremors across her belly as his lips touched the sensitive skin there.

And then she felt as though she might melt from sheer ecstasy as he stood and bent his head low, flicking his tongue across the nipple of one of her breasts. He transferred his attention to the other, his hands cupping her breasts, lovingly cradling them.

"What are you doing to me?" Shirleen said in whisper, arching her back in invitation. She reached up and twined her fingers through her hair, lifting it from her shoulders, then let it fall back down again.

"I have never felt anything like this," she murmured.

"There is so much more to feel," Blue Thunder said, fully standing now and slowly turning her so that her back was to him.

She gasped with the wonder of it when Blue Thunder began gently kissing her scars, first one and then another, making her feel something far different from the pain that had come when they were inflicted.

As Blue Thunder's tongue licked each scar so lovingly, Shirleen could not help crying softly at the thought that this man could love her so much, even though she had been so terribly scarred by a madman.

And then he turned her to face him.

She brushed the tears away as she watched him slowly disrobe until his magnificently muscled body was revealed to her eyes in its total nude splendor!

She could not help herself.

She reached out and moved her hand over his muscled arms, his powerful shoulders, and then his hairless, muscled chest.

She saw how the touch of her fingers made his hard body tremble. When she came to that part of him that proved his sex, she blushed at how God had bestowed him with such power even there!

She had only seen one man nude.

Earl.

And he was nothing in comparison.

His manhood was small, sort of wrinkled and shriveled, whereas Blue Thunder's was, oh, so much larger!

"Touch me there, too," Blue Thunder said, reaching for her hand and placing it on his throbbing member. "Caress me there."

Having never tried such a thing before, yet strangely tempted by the thought of doing it, Shirleen gazed bashfully into his eyes. As she slowly wrapped her fingers around him, his heat against her flesh made her eyes widen.

"Move your hand on me," Blue Thunder encouraged. "For a moment, and then I want to be inside you. I want you to know the gentleness of a man, yet the full pleasure that a man who loves you can give to you."

Feeling as though she were living a dream, hoping that someone would not suddenly awaken her, she began moving her hand on him. His body shuddered and his eyes closed, making her realize that she was giving him the same sort of pleasure his hands and tongue had given her.

She stroked him for another moment; then he reached down and took her hand away.

He drew her hard against him and enfolded her within his powerful arms. He lowered his lips to hers and kissed her passionately as he used his body to press her down onto the plush pelts and blankets on the lodge floor.

As she lay there on her back, she gazed up at him through a haze of sexual wanting.

He blanketed her with his body, and as he kissed her again, he thrust the magnificent length of his manhood deep within her. Each of his rhythmic strokes brought a newfound ecstasy to Shirleen's pounding heart.

She sought his mouth with a wildness that was also new to her and kissed him as she twined her arms around his neck and clung to him, almost desperately, meeting each of his thrusts with abandon.

She was clinging, floating, laughing, and crying all at the same time as he rained kisses on her lids and on her hair. His own pleasure was building inexorably within him as he drove into her swiftly, surely.

Shirleen was very aware now of the urgency of his mouth and hands as he again took her mouth by storm, his palms moving seductively over her.

"Please . . . please . . ." Shirleen heard herself say. She was not even sure what she was pleading for, because he was doing everything wonderfully right as far as she was concerned.

He was making certain that she was receiving pleasure, just as she was giving it back to him.

"My woman, how I do love you," Blue Thunder whispered against her parted lips.

"As I do you," Shirleen whispered back.

And then he kissed her again.

With a moan of ecstasy, she gave him back the kiss, clinging, moving as he moved, and opening herself more widely to him so that she could feel him even deeper within her.

Blue Thunder could hardly hold back the final throes of ecstasy, for his whole body was on fire with a passion he had never known possible.

But now? While he was with Shirleen? It seemed that everything that had lain dormant within him for so long had awoken. He felt like a true man!

He felt the passion mounting, cresting, and exploding, his body quivering hard into hers as her pleasure matched his. She clung, moaned, and moved in time with his pounding thrusts.

And then it was over.

They both lay breathing hard and clinging to one another.

Their yearnings, their hunger for each other, had been fed.

Blue Thunder felt that he was ready to go and conquer the world for this woman he would always love!

But he knew there was only one thing that needed to be achieved this day. He had to rescue his woman's daughter.

Shirleen was suddenly aware of movement outside the tepee.

Horses.

She knew that the warriors were taking their steeds from their corrals and readying themselves for travel. She could envision Speckled Fawn on her steed, ready to help rescue Shirleen's precious Megan.

"I wish I could go with you," Shirleen said. She sat up and pulled a soft blanket around her shoulders as she watched Blue Thunder quickly don his fringed buckskin clothing, and then his fringed moccasins.

She stood up, and the blanket fell to the floor around her feet. She wove her fingers through the thick locks of his hair, straightening it so the strands hung long and smooth down his back.

He swept his arms around her waist and drew her powerfully to him. "It is best that you stay and wait for your daughter to be brought to you," he said hoarsely. "And I promise you that she will be with you, soon."

She clung to his neck and pressed her cheek to his powerful chest, the buckskin of his shirt soft against her face. "I will miss you so," she murmured, near tears. "I will pray for you and your warriors, and also for Speckled Fawn, the dear, courageous woman that she is."

"I will take the memory of what we just shared with me," Blue Thunder said, his eyes twinkling as he gazed down into hers. "Those memories will sustain me until we are together again in our blankets. My woman, I say to you that this will be soon. Your daughter will be sleeping near us in her own nest of blankets in this lodge. We will hang a blanket to secure both her privacy and ours when it comes time to go to our beds."

"I will hold on to that thought while you are gone," Shirleen said, smiling into his eyes.

"Dress, my woman, so that you can see me off," Blue Thunder said, hurrying to his cache of weapons.

As Shirleen dressed, Blue Thunder sheathed a knife at his waist.

Then he grabbed up his rifle and returned to Shirleen, who was now fully clothed.

"I am ready," she said softly. "I will try not to allow myself to worry too much while you are gone."

"Worrying is for the weak," Blue Thunder said firmly. "And, woman, you are anything but weak." His eyes roamed slowly over her; then he chuckled as he gazed into her eyes again. "You might be tiny, but you are not weak. You have proven to me that you are a woman of much passion . . . much courage."

She blushed and laughed softly, then left the tepee with him.

Just as he started to mount his steed, which

had been readied for him by a small brave whose role it was to tend to Blue Thunder's horses, someone came running up to him.

Blue Thunder turned and gazed at Moon Star, the woman who had been left in charge of Dancing Shadow while Speckled Fawn was away. Then he looked at Speckled Fawn, who was already mounted on her steed beside Blue Thunder's.

"What is it?" Blue Thunder and Speckled Fawn said in almost the same breath.

"Dancing Shadow has taken a turn for the worse," Moon Star said, and a strange silence fell suddenly all around her.

Chapter Twenty-one

As sweet and musical
As bright Apollo's lute,
Strung with his hair,
And when love speaks,
The voice of all the gods
Makes heaven drowsy with the harmony.
—SHAKESPEARE

The news had rendered everyone silent. Of course they had known that Dancing Shadow could not live much longer, but the fact that he had worsened tore at each of their hearts.

Even Shirleen felt a deep sadness, for although she had never known Dancing Shadow except by reputation, she knew that his passing would bring much sadness into the village.

Without further hesitation, Speckled Fawn hurried toward her home. Shirleen and Blue Thunder walked quickly behind her.

When they arrived at the lodge, they stopped, then quietly crept inside together. The sun filtered peacefully through the smoke hole overhead, looking mystical as the slowly rising smoke from the lodge fire bled into it.

Shirleen stayed just inside the lodge door while Blue Thunder and Speckled Fawn went to kneel at Dancing Shadow's side.

Speckled Fawn stifled a sob behind a hand as she gazed down at her husband, lying there so motionless. She had seen him like this several times before, and she hoped this occasion was no different from the last. Then he had also seemed to take a turn for the worse, but awoke a few hours later, smiling. He was once more his usual quiet self, not ready to die just yet.

"I believe it is the same as before," Blue Thunder said, placing a gentle hand on his uncle's brow, which was cool to the touch.

He looked over at Speckled Fawn. He saw deep concern in her eyes, proving once again how much she loved her elderly husband.

"Speckled Fawn, I believe your husband is in one of his deep sleeps," he explained. "I do not believe that he will die anytime soon because I have seen this many times before, just as you have. He slides peacefully into a sleeping stage such as he is in now, but awakens none the worse for it."

"But, my chief, we cannot be sure," Speckled Fawn said, reaching out to smooth the blanket that was spread over her husband.

She turned to Blue Thunder. "I truly do not know what to do," she said, searching his eyes for answers. "What if this is not one of those sleeps? What if he does not awaken this time? You know as well as I do that it is going to happen one of these days. He . . . is . . . not at all well."

"You must do what your heart tells you to do," Blue Thunder said thickly. "But remember this, Speckled Fawn: A child's life hangs in the balance. I do not doubt that at all. If we do not carry out today the plan we have made to rescue her, we may lose any opportunity to do so. If the child's father leaves with her on a riverboat, she will disappear from her mother's life forever."

Speckled Fawn lowered her eyes.

Tears streamed down her cheeks.

In her mind's eye she was seeing the scars on Shirleen's back. She believed that the man who had caused them would eventually do the same to his daughter, if not worse.

Oh, good Lord above, she did not know what to do.

She had told her husband she would be there for him always. Yet she had promised Shirleen she would go and help rescue Megan.

She weighed both promises inside her heart and realized that the child must come first. She still had a long life ahead of her, whereas Speckled Fawn's husband had had his life, a wonderful one as his people's shaman.

Knowing what she must do, what her heart prompted her to do, Speckled Fawn stood quickly and went to Shirleen.

She took both of Shirleen's hands in hers. "Will you sit with my husband while I am gone?" she asked, trying to hide her conflicting emotions. She did not want Shirleen to know just how difficult was this decision she had made.

She did not want Shirleen to think she would

go to rescue Megan with only half a heart.
Speckled Fawn wanted to look strong.

She wanted Shirleen to believe that soon she
would see her daughter again!

Shirleen could hear the neighing of horses
just outside the lodge. They belonged to the
men who waited for their chief to depart for Fort
Dennison.

Then she was keenly aware of voices talking
softly, also outside the lodge.

She knew that the entire village had heard
how Dancing Shadow had gone into a deep,
silent sleep. The people of the Wind Band had
come to pay their respects, if necessary.

She knew that everyone loved this old man
and would do anything for him, as well as for
his wife Speckled Fawn. They all knew how
dutiful and loving she had been to him since
their marriage.

Shirleen knew that while Speckled Fawn
was away from the village, helping to rescue
sweet Megan, she would not be alone while she
sat at the elder's side. The entire village would
be there, just outside the lodge.

"I will sit with him and care for him while
you are gone," Shirleen said. She felt the
strength in Speckled Fawn's arms as she flung
them around Shirleen's neck, hugging her.

"Thank you," Speckled Fawn murmured.
She stepped away from Shirleen, but still held
her hands. "Know this, Shirleen. I will do
everything I can to rescue your daughter from
that madman. And I know that it must be

done in haste, for once that man is on the riverboat, there will be no way of stopping him. I cannot allow Megan to be lost to you forever."

Shirleen hugged the other woman almost desperately. "I shall forever be grateful," she sobbed. "Thank you, thank you."

"We must go now," Speckled Fawn said, stepping away from Shirleen.

She turned to Blue Thunder, who was now standing beside her husband's bed. "I will be ready as soon as I give my husband a kiss and explain to him what I am going to do. Although he cannot hear me, he will understand. He would want me to leave, to help rescue a child. He has always loved children so much. He would have been a good father."

"While serving his people as shaman, he never gave in to his desires to have a wife. His duties to his people always came first with him," Blue Thunder said, going to her. "You gave him what he never had. You are a good woman, Speckled Fawn. I am sorry if I have made you uncomfortable at times. I know now what a very good woman you are. You were a perfect choice for my uncle."

"You have no idea how I appreciate what you are saying," Speckled Fawn said, wiping tears from her face. "I hope after we return from the fort that you will have another reason to think highly of me. I am determined to help get Megan away from that horrible man and bring her back to the loving arms of her mother."

"We shall do that together," Blue Thunder said fervently.

He stepped aside. "Speckled Fawn, say good-bye to your husband, for we must leave immediately."

Then as Speckled Fawn knelt to speak to Dancing Shadow, Blue Thunder went to Shirleen and drew her into his gentle embrace.

"Do not despair while we are gone," he whispered into her ear. "Soon you will have your daughter back with you. I promise you, my woman, that I will see to it."

"I have no doubt that I will have Megan with me again, because I know the strength of your word, as well as Speckled Fawn's," Shirleen said. She clung almost desperately to this man who was going to be putting himself and his warriors into danger for her daughter's sake.

She knew that he thought it wise to avoid fighting and confrontation with whites at all costs. The fact that he was risking everything for her and Megan touched her heart deeply.

She would not allow herself to feel guilty for having pulled this wonderful young chief into a possible confrontation with the cavalry.

But, how she dreaded the fact that her beloved would be riding into danger. "I will pray for you and Speckled Fawn and my daughter until your return," she murmured.

She eased herself from his arms and turned to gaze down at Speckled Fawn, who was leaning over Dancing Shadow and giving him one last parting kiss.

Shirleen was deeply moved by the sight of the love that Speckled Fawn had for her elderly husband.

Speckled Fawn rose to her feet and came to Blue Thunder and Shirleen. "I am ready," she said firmly. "I have said good-bye to my husband. I . . . I . . . truly believe that he, somehow, heard me."

She turned to Shirleen and gazed intently into her eyes. "Thank you for sitting with my husband in my absence," she said.

"I just can't thank you enough for what you are doing for me and my daughter," Shirleen said softly. "And believe me when I say that while you are gone, I will not leave your husband's side."

They hugged, and then Blue Thunder and Speckled Fawn departed. Shirleen did not even step out of the tepee long enough to watch them ride away, for she did not want to leave Dancing Shadow unattended for even a moment.

She hurried to him and sat down on the soft mats beside the bed of pelts.

Soon Shirleen heard the thundering of hooves and knew that Blue Thunder and Speckled Fawn would be riding side by side, while the warriors followed behind them.

She knew that many hides would be tied to the packhorses, to be offered for trade. This trading was the reason that would be given the sentries to get Blue Thunder and his men into the fort.

Shirleen smiled as she thought of how Speckled Fawn was dressed for her role in this plot. Speckled Fawn was not wearing her usual Indian attire today. Instead, she was dressed in some of the clothes that had been stolen by the renegades.

She would look the part of a distraught white woman who'd lost everything but her life at the hand of renegades.

Knowing she had many hours to wait before she would learn whether Megan had been saved from her abusive madman of a father, Shirleen tried to focus on the elderly sleeping man.

She took his hand and gently held it. She hoped that if he felt her hand in his while he slept, he might believe it was his wife's.

She did not speak, for if he was aware of things at all, he would realize that the voice was not his wife's.

Instead, she began humming.

She remembered how her mama long ago had sat beside the elderly people of her church when they became gravely ill, humming to them.

Her mother had said that if nothing else could reach inside the heart of those who were near death, soft music might.

Shirleen's eyes widened, for if she wasn't wrong, Dancing Shadow had just given a fleeting smile.

She smiled too, glad in the belief that she was helping this old man in at least a small way.

She continued humming church hymns, trying to remember the songs she had heard her mama humming.

"The Old Rugged Cross" had been her mama's favorite.

She began humming it, for perhaps it would become Dancing Shadow's favorite, too.

Although she was doing what she could to keep busy in her hours of crisis, Shirleen could not stop wondering about whether she would ever see her child again.

Oh, surely she would!

Had not Blue Thunder promised her that it would be so?

Chapter Twenty-two

Serene I fold my arms and wait.
—Burroughs

After seeing that Speckled Fawn was well hidden in the trees outside Fort Dennison, Blue Thunder and his warriors rode onward toward the tall walls of the fort, their packhorses heavily laden with plush pelts.

After arriving at the gates of the fort, Blue Thunder and his men stopped, except for two who approached the two white sentries standing guard.

Blue Thunder sat stiffly in his saddle as he waited for his warriors to do their normal report to the sentries of how many warriors were in their party, and how many skins were being brought for trade.

Although this was the routine whenever they came to the fort for trade, Blue Thunder's jaw tightened. Today they had much more to accomplish than trade.

Once inside the walls of the fort, he would

have to behave normally, bargaining for supplies in exchange for his furs, while his mind and eyes would be on other things.

While exchanging small talk as well as food and smokes with the colonel in charge, Blue Thunder would be watching for a blond-haired, blue-eyed man who fit the description of his woman's husband, as well as the child who was reported to be with him.

He hoped the plan would all go smoothly, for he did not want to return to his home, or Shirleen, empty-handed.

Still waiting, and observing what was happening at the closed gates, he saw one of the pony soldiers hand over a packet of tobacco, which would be brought to Blue Thunder with an invitation for his party to proceed into the fort. Even now the gates were being opened as his warriors rode back toward him.

Proud Horse came up beside Blue Thunder, stopped, then handed over the buckskin packet of tobacco.

"We are welcome to trade," Proud Horse said quietly. "But I have news, and I am not sure whether it is good or bad."

"And what news is this?" Blue Thunder asked as he took the tobacco packet and tied its drawstrings to the waistband of his fringed breeches.

"I think the news is good, and I believe you will think so, too," Proud Horse said, slowly smiling. "My chief, there is a new colonel in charge of Fort Dennison, replacing the one who has been known to say he would proudly spit on all Indians if he had the chance. The young sentry who gave me the tobacco seemed proud to say that the new colonel is one who is kind and who strives for peace."

"That is good . . . if it is true," Blue Thunder replied, always skeptical of news that was said to be good and should make the red man happy.

He had heard of such tricks before, of leaders who were said to be good-hearted toward Indians, and then killed and even scalped them at the first opportunity.

"His name is?" Blue Thunder asked. He was proud to know many of the colonels in charge, who traveled from one fort to another.

"Colonel Cline," Proud Horse said. "Colonel Harold Cline."

"It is a kindly sounding name, though not one I know. I hope the man himself is kind as well," Blue Thunder said. He turned to address his other warriors. "We have been given an invitation to enter the fort walls. We shall go in now. But you know what role you must play while we are there, besides making a good trade. You are to watch for a white man such as Shirleen described to us. Also notice whether a white child of my daughter's age is with this man."

Everyone nodded, and then Blue Thunder pointed the way forward and they all rode into the fort. Since Blue Thunder was a well-known and admired chief who strived for peace with white people at all times, he was greeted with the usual recognition of such a leader. The American flag was raised and cannons were fired to announce his arrival.

The first time that had happened, Blue Thunder had been alarmed by the pony soldiers' response. He had thought he was being mocked and was riding into the face of danger.

But after he'd heard the commander's explanation of the salute, he had realized that he should be proud of such a greeting, not angry, afraid, or suspicious.

Now he smiled and nodded at the soldier who was raising the flag, and then at the one who had fired the cannon.

Trusting the white pony soldiers' intentions, and also having faith in the commander whom Blue Thunder had not yet met face-to-face, he rode on inside the fort walls. His warriors and their heavily laden packhorses followed him.

Once they were all inside, several soldiers came and saluted them, then led them on foot to a large outdoor receiving area.

There the horses were unpacked and each warrior took charge of his own skins, placing them on tables for the trading that would come after food and smokes were shared with the new colonel.

Having brought no pelts of his own, Blue Thunder dismounted and led his horse over to where many of the pony soldiers' steeds were lined up along a hitching rail.

As he wrapped his reins around the rail, he heard heavy footsteps coming up behind him.

He turned on a moccasined heel and found himself face-to-face with the new colonel, who wore a freshly ironed blue uniform with shining brass buttons that reflected the rays of the late afternoon sun.

His face was square-jawed, his black hair was sprinkled with gray, and his eyes were of a violet color that Blue Thunder had never seen before.

But it was the man's smile and firm handshake that told Blue Thunder that what he had heard about the new commander was true. His eyes shone with kindness as he smiled at Blue Thunder, his hand now lowering away from Blue Thunder's to rest on a sheathed saber at his right side.

"Welcome to Fort Dennison," Colonel Cline said, smiling broadly and revealing a smooth line of sparkling white teeth. "I have heard about you. It is good to finally make your acquaintance."

"It is good to make yours," Blue Thunder replied. He walked with the colonel toward a large table that sat away from the other tables where the pelts and robes were being neatly displayed.

As they sat down opposite one another, so that Blue Thunder would have a full view of the bargaining that was to take place, food was brought to the table and plates were stacked for those who wished to eat.

"I hope you will enjoy the feast I offer you and your warriors today," Colonel Cline said, also watching the Assiniboine warriors unload their packhorses. When they had finished, they came with some of the soldiers and were offered places at the table.

"You are kind to offer such a feast," Blue Thunder said as he eyed the platters piled high with venison meat, fruit, vegetables, and bread. "*Pila-maye.*"

He smelled the familiar aroma of the black drink called coffee, which had become one of the usual offerings at a time of trade.

And then a soldier brought a wrapped pipe and handed it the colonel.

Blue Thunder watched as the colonel unwrapped the red cloth, revealing a beautifully feathered, long-stemmed pipe.

"This was a gift given to me by a Cheyenne chief some time ago after a peace treaty was signed between us," Colonel Cline said. He shook tobacco from a leather drawstring bag into the lovely painted bowl of the pipe. "Smoke with me. It will seal our friendship and future trades."

Blue Thunder hoped that he hid his uneasiness and resentment at the sight of the pipe. Such a gift, after a peace treaty was signed, was supposed to seal the friendship which had resulted in peace. In reality, most of the time those treaties had been broken by whites and the gift of the pipe was made a mockery.

Knowing that he had no choice but to take a smoke from the pipe or insult this new white leader, Blue Thunder accepted it.

He held the long stem and took one long drag from the pipe, quickly inhaling the smoke, then returned the pipe to the colonel. He watched as Colonel Cline smoked from the same pipe stem, exhaling the smoke much more slowly as his eyes met and held Blue Thunder's.

And then, that quickly, that part of the ceremony was over.

Then the feast began.

Many white soldiers came and sat at the same table as Blue Thunder and his warriors. They laughed and ate and seemed sincere in their kindness toward their visitors.

But all the time that Blue Thunder sat and ate, his eyes were never still.

He looked over his shoulder, and then straight ahead, and then glanced to one side and another, as other white people, both uniformed and not, came to look at the rich pelts and robes that had been brought for trade.

Suddenly Blue Thunder's heart skipped a beat when he spied a man with golden hair worn to his waist, and piercing blue eyes. He held a small girl in his arms . . . a child who perfectly fit Megan's description.

She had wrapped one tiny arm around the man's neck, and in her blue eyes there was such sadness!

Blue Thunder did not want to attract the attention of the colonel or any of the other soldiers at the table. He had to be subtle in his observation of the man.

The golden-haired man moved slowly down the line of long tables piled high with items for trade.

Trading was the last thing on Blue Thunder's mind as he tried not to stare at the white man and child. He must not draw suspicion toward himself, or their plan might be jeopardized.

So he finished the food on his plate, as did everyone else, and then the white and red-skinned men rose from the table and the bargaining commenced.

As the white people made their choices, Blue Thunder stood back with the colonel, awaiting the time when his warriors would receive their payment in the large room where supplies were kept. Then each would choose the items he wished to take home to his wife.

When the colonel excused himself after a soldier came with news that required his attention, Blue Thunder seized this opportunity to approach the white man he'd been surreptitiously watching. He sidled up next to him and walked along the tables beside him.

Surprisingly, the white man stopped and turned to Blue Thunder, who was known far and wide as a good and peaceful chief.

"Good afternoon, Chief," Earl said, a glint in his blue eyes as he gazed at Blue Thunder.

"Mighty fine pelts you and your warriors have brought for trade." He reached his hand out toward Blue Thunder for a handshake. "Earl. Earl Mingus is my name, and this here is my sweet daughter Megan."

Now that he knew for certain that he was face-to-face with Shirleen's husband and her pretty, sweet daughter, for a moment Blue Thunder could not find his voice to respond.

Quickly pulling himself together, Blue Thunder took Earl's hand and politely shook it. "Yes, the trade is good today," he said, but he removed his hand as soon as he could without letting on that the very touch of this man's flesh filled Blue Thunder with loathing.

Blue Thunder turned his attention elsewhere. He smiled at Megan, whose eyes showed anything but happiness. "Your child is how many winters old?" he asked.

He was trying to think of a way to carry on a conversation with the man until he could get away from him. Now that he knew Earl and Megan were in Fort Dennison, he was to contact Speckled Fawn so their plan could proceed.

He was anxious to get this accomplished so that he could return to the safety of his village with the little girl who showed fear in her beautiful blue eyes . . . fear of her very own *ahte*.

Earl gazed at Blue Thunder as he raised an eyebrow. "What did you just ask me? What does it mean . . . how many winters?"

"Your daughter's age," Blue Thunder said,

smiling to himself at this man's ignorance of Indian terms. "You see, I have a daughter who might be the same age."

"My Megan is four years old," Earl replied, a hint of mockery in his voice.

"And do you have a wife?" Blue Thunder asked, wondering just how this man would choose to lie to him.

"There are only my daughter and myself waiting for a paddlewheeler that will take us away from this godforsaken place," Earl said. He was suddenly aware of a glint of hatred in the chief's eyes and wondered what had caused it, especially since it was rumored that this particular chief was friendly to white people.

Not really caring, Earl excused himself and hurried away. He didn't notice that one of Blue Thunder's warriors followed him.

Just as Earl walked away, the colonel returned.

Blue Thunder turned to him and shook his hand. "It has been a good trade, a good time of camaraderie," Blue Thunder said pleasantly. "But now it is time for me and my warriors to return to our homes. Thank you for the generous food, drink, and smoke. My warriors and I will return later in the fall with even better and thicker pelts for trading."

"You do not wish to spend the night?" Colonel Cline asked as he slowly took his hand away. "It is the custom, you know, for me to offer the chief a night's lodging in my home while the warriors sleep in the courtyard."

"I know, and I thank you for the invitation, but I have an ailing uncle who awaits my return," Blue Thunder said. Although that was true, Blue Thunder had another reason for making such a quick retreat from the fort. Speckled Fawn awaited his return with news of whether the white man was there with the child.

"I am sorry about your uncle," Colonel Cline said, walking Blue Thunder to his horse. "Will you give him my best?"

"I shall do that," Blue Thunder answered, untying the reins as his warriors also prepared their horses for travel, strapping the goods they'd acquired onto the backs of their packhorses.

They all mounted their steeds and rode slowly through the courtyard, then out the wide gate.

Short Robe, the warrior who had followed Earl to learn which cabin was his for the night, soon joined them. He smiled at Blue Thunder. "The dwelling and its location will be easily described to Speckled Fawn," he said. "Thus far, the plan seems to be working, do you not think so?"

"It is not wise to become too confident about such things," Blue Thunder replied. "We must still proceed with much caution, and so should Speckled Fawn."

Soon they entered the dark shadows of the forest, where Speckled Fawn awaited their return, and told her the good news, that the child was there for the taking. They were then forced to wait several hours so that Speckled Fawn's arrival would not be connected with the Assiniboine's visit.

When the sun began to lower toward the horizon, Blue Thunder stepped up to Speckled Fawn, and as was planned, he ripped the skirt of her dress, mussed up her hair, and smeared dirt on her face.

When that was done, he held her hands in his. "Are you ready?" he asked as he searched her eyes. "Do you still feel confident about our plan?"

Smiling broadly, Speckled Fawn raised her skirt and patted the knife sheathed at her right thigh. "Here is my confidence," she said smartly. "Just stay here, close to the fort, so that I will not have to run too far when I escape with the child."

She and Blue Thunder embraced one another.

And then she left.

Although she had not admitted it to Blue Thunder, Speckled Fawn was actually terrified.

She focused all her energy on playing the role she had undertaken. She faked a limp and made herself look distraught as she walked in the direction of the fort.

When she finally came into view of the sentries at the gate, she pretended to stumble even worse and began screaming for help.

The sentries ran to her.

They stood on each side of her and took her gently by her elbows to hold her steady as she told them she was the only survivor of an Indian massacre. She told how murdering renegades had attacked her homestead; how she had walked for many miles to get to the fort.

She begged for their help.

She was quickly reassured and taken inside.

Speckled Fawn had never been much of a praying woman, but at this moment, she whispered a prayer that all would go well. If Earl saw through her act, both she and Megan would be doomed.

Chapter Twenty-three

Now summon the red current to thine heart—
Old man, thy mightiest woe remains to tell.
                                        —Anonymous

The hours seemed to stretch out interminably as Shirleen waited for Blue Thunder to return. She was no longer humming or singing to the old, ailing shaman. He had not awakened, not even for one minute, as she sat there.

And she had noticed at times how shallowly he was breathing. Sometimes he stopped breathing for a moment or two, and then resumed again.

During those moments when he was not breathing, Shirleen had been filled with a cold panic, expecting him to die at any time. If he died while she was with him, would his people somehow blame her?

Would they possibly blame Speckled Fawn for not remaining dutifully at his bedside, leaving another woman there in her stead?

Oh, Lord, Shirleen hoped neither of them

would be blamed. Speckled Fawn was forfeiting her time with her husband in order to save an innocent child!

Shirleen's child!

She cast another glance over her shoulder at the closed entrance flap.

Often today she had heard the hide flutter, causing her to believe someone was entering the tepee, only to find each time that it was only the wind.

Outside the tepee most of the villagers stood vigil, awaiting news about Dancing Shadow.

Shirleen had gone to the flap several times to lift it aside and tell the people that their beloved Dancing Shadow still slept peacefully.

And that was so.

Except for those brief moments when his breathing stopped, the old shaman seemed to be at peace.

She turned and gazed at Dancing Shadow as he continued to sleep.

She studied his wrinkled face.

Surely at one time he had been everything to his people.

But now he awaited death alone, as every man must.

Sighing, Shirleen rose and went to the entranceway. She held the flap aside and gave a reassuring smile to the people who still stood there, awaiting news of the beloved old man.

The day had been long.

Most of those who had stood there waiting

had returned to their homes, to share the evening meal with their families.

Shirleen could even now smell the cooked venison and corn.

Only moments ago, Bright Sun had brought Shirleen a platter of food, then left.

Shirleen found it hard even to think of eating. She had so much on her mind that she felt a little queasy.

The ailing shaman.

Shirleen's daughter.

Blue Thunder.

Speckled Fawn.

What were Blue Thunder and Speckled Fawn doing at this very moment?

Had their plan worked?

Sitting as she had for so long now beside the old shaman, Shirleen had lost track of time.

She stared into the distance, where a sunset flared red along the horizon.

She wished that she could have gone with Blue Thunder and Speckled Fawn, but knew her presence would only have complicated matters if she'd been noticed.

Shirleen's heart skipped a beat when she heard a weak voice speaking behind her. It . . . had to be . . .

"Dancing Shadow," Shirleen whispered as she turned to the old man.

"Speckled Fawn," he whispered, holding out a trembling hand to Shirleen.

She realized that he thought his wife was in

his lodge with him, not someone he had never met. Shirleen desperately wished that it were Speckled Fawn instead of herself that the old man was gazing at so intently.

Surprised that he was actually talking, and so glad that he was awake, Shirleen rushed to his bedside and knelt beside it.

Dancing Shadow squinted his old, faded eyes as he stared at Shirleen, then again reached his frail, quivering hand toward her. "Speckled Fawn?" he said, almost too softly for Shirleen to understand.

She sat down beside the bed of pelts and blankets just as the old, shaky hand reached higher and touched her hair.

"My beautiful wife, it is good to see your hair a flame color again," Dancing Shadow said, pausing between every other word to catch his breath. "That was the color of your hair when I first saw you."

Shirleen was now absolutely certain that he thought she was Speckled Fawn. She was stunned that he seemed to be partly rational, and was even speaking. She had been told that he had not spoken for a long time.

Oh, how she wished that Speckled Fawn and Blue Thunder were there to hear the old man finally speaking. And he had not said only one or two words, but full sentences.

He was even aware of the color of her hair.

Yet he still had not recognized that he was not talking with his wife, but someone who was a total stranger to him.

Hoping to make him happy in his last moments, Shirleen tried her best to pretend to be Speckled Fawn. She lowered her voice, making it gruffy and scratchy sounding as she responded to Dancing Shadow.

"My husband, I am so glad you are awake," Shirleen said.

She took his hand in hers, trying not to show her alarm at how cold his flesh was.

She recalled that when one of her aunts lay dying some years ago, and Shirleen had come to say her final good-bye, the coldness of her aunt's withered hand had sent spirals of dread into Shirleen's heart. She had realized then that her aunt was near death.

Did the coldness of this elderly man's hand mean the same?

Was Shirleen going to witness another death? Her Aunt Sara had died while clutching Shirleen's hand.

She recalled with a strange sort of horror how as soon as her aunt took her last breath, her hand had tightened around Shirleen's. She'd had a hard time getting her hand free from her aunt's grip.

When her mother had come and helped her, Shirleen had rushed from the room, crying. Even her father's comforting arms had not erased that moment from her mind.

"My husband, I have missed you so much," Shirleen murmured, glancing off and on at his hand, which seemed to be clutching hers harder by the moment.

He had been so happy to be able to touch her hair again, believing he was touching his wife's.

She smiled at him although it was the last thing she felt like doing. She was terrified that he was dying right before her eyes!

She tried to think past that. "I am so glad that you like the color of my hair," she said, her voice catching as Dancing Shadow closed his eyes and held them closed for a long time. What if he never opened them again? What if he did die while she was alone with him?

When he opened his eyes and again smiled weakly at her, Shirleen sucked in a breath of relief. "I . . . dyed . . . it red again just for you," she lied.

His old eyes twinkled, he chuckled, and then his eyes went wild as he yanked his hand from Shirleen's and clutched hard at his chest.

To Shirleen's horror, he was suddenly dead, his eyes now fixed in a death stare. Fortunately, his gaze was locked on something past her and not on her face. But she suddenly realized that what his eyes were staring at was the least of her worries.

What was she to do?

Would Blue Thunder's people blame her?

Oh, no!

They couldn't!

She was only sitting with Dancing Shadow. She had kept her promise to Speckled Fawn. She had not left his side. She had done her best to make his last moments peaceful.

She had sung to him.

She had even held his hand!

Knowing that she had no choice but to reveal his death to everyone, she rose shakily to her feet.

She sucked in a deep breath as she tried to gather enough courage to face whatever lay ahead of her.

Then she went and held the entrance flap aside.

She saw that most people had returned to stand outside Dancing Shadow's tepee after they had finished their evening meals.

They were staring at her questioningly.

She wondered if they could see the fear on her face?

She wondered if they could see that she was trembling uncontrollably.

She finally gulped out that Dancing Shadow had just taken his last breath of life.

"But . . . but . . . he spoke to me before he died," she quickly added. "He . . . was happy. He smiled just moments before he died!"

Aunt Bright Sun stepped from the crowd and came to Shirleen. She took Shirleen gently by the elbow and led her back to Blue Thunder's tepee. All the while, Little Bee followed, hanging on to Bright Sun's buckskin skirt.

"I have kept Blue Thunder's fire going in his absence," Bright Sun said. "Sit beside it. I shall sit with you."

Little Bee sat between Bright Sun and

Shirleen, quietly playing with her doll, oblivious of the loss of Dancing Shadow.

"Shirleen, no one holds you to blame for our loved one's death," Bright Sun said reassuringly when she noticed the frightened look in Shirleen's eyes. She reached over and gently patted her face. "In fact, my people thank you for sitting with Dancing Shadow in the absence of his wife."

"Thank you for letting me know that," Shirleen murmured. She wiped tears from her eyes. "I am filled with so many emotions. I am so torn. I feel bad for Dancing Shadow, and I . . . I . . . am in constant fear for my daughter's welfare. If anything should happen to her—"

"Do not imagine the worst," Bright Sun said. "When Blue Thunder sets his mind on doing something, he always comes out the victor."

"I truly hope that is the case this time," Shirleen said. She sighed heavily and hung her head as tears filled her eyes again. "It is almost too much for me to bear. I shall never forget those last moments with Dancing Shadow."

She raised her eyes and looked through her tears at Bright Sun. "I . . . can't help . . . being afraid that something might go awry at the fort and Blue Thunder and Speckled Fawn could be harmed," she blurted out.

"Blue Thunder is a very wise man, wise past his young years as chief," Bright Sun again reassured her. "He is his father's son, and his father was one of the greatest leaders of our

Assiniboine people. Blue Thunder's intelligence and ability as a leader will bring him home to us, along with Speckled Fawn. Your daughter will be with them. I saw it in the clouds today as I looked up at them. The clouds tell me many things. Today they gave me comfort that I wish to pass along to you."

"Thank you so much for the kind words of encouragement," Shirleen said, in awe of the woman's ability to see and know things that surely no one else saw.

Shirleen was discovering that the Assiniboine were a people ruled by mysticism, which brought them faith and guidance in their everyday lives.

Shirleen looked down at Little Bee as she crawled trustingly onto her lap. As the child leaned her cheek against Shirleen's bosom, Little Bee fell asleep.

The innocent action of the little girl made Shirleen ache even more to have her own daughter with her.

She became suddenly aware of drums pounding out a dirge outside the tepee; people's voices blended as they began openly mourning their departed loved one.

She now felt blessed for those few last moments with a man whom so many had loved. In that short time while he was awake and smiling at her, he had shown her just why he was so beloved by his Assiniboine people!

She no longer felt afraid that she would

somehow be blamed for his death. She now knew that these people saw something mystical even in death.

She hoped that she, too, would react to the world in the way of these wonderful people when she became the wife of their young chief.

The thought of becoming Blue Thunder's wife made her time awaiting his return bearable.

When he came back to the village, she had no doubt that he would have Megan with him!

Chapter Twenty-four

Who is this happy warrior?
Who is he that every man in arms
Should wish to be?

—Wordsworth

Speckled Fawn still pretended to stumble as she was taken to a cabin by two soldiers. It was scarcely furnished and . . . there were bars on its only window.

The bars made her heart skip a beat as she was led to the small bed beneath the window.

Had she stepped into a trap? Had the colonel of this fort discovered what she had come for?

Had someone been spying on Blue Thunder and his warriors?

If so, had she been seen with them?

Now she feared not only for herself, but also for Blue Thunder and those brave warriors with him.

Perhaps even now the soldiers were with Blue Thunder, arresting or killing him for making plans against a white settler.

"Please excuse us for bringing you here. There is no other available lodging," a soldier with brilliant red hair said as he helped Speckled Fawn down to the cot, which had a mattress on it but nothing more. "You will be brought clean sheets, a basin of water, and a clean dress. My wife will bring you one to wear. She is the same size as you, so the dress should fit you well enough."

It was as though a fresh breeze of air had swept into the room. Speckled Fawn realized that her immediate fears were unfounded. She was not being arrested.

"I appreciate what you are doing for me," Speckled Fawn said, easing herself down onto the mattress and trying to ignore the smell of urine on it. She hated to imagine just who had slept on it, for surely the worst of criminals were brought to this cell until they were taken elsewhere for their punishment.

If she had been captured years ago when she was on the run after stabbing a rapist to death, she could have been made to stay in such a desolate, stinking cabin.

As it was, she would not even spend a full night there. As soon as she managed to get the child, she would flee into the night.

"My name's Jack. What's yours?" the red-haired man asked, looking intently at her.

For a moment a chill rushed down Speckled Fawn's spine.

This man was looking at her so carefully, as though he were studying her features. Did it mean that he remembered her from somewhere . . . perhaps a Wanted poster?

But she scoffed at that idea. She had seen one of the posters, and the drawing had been nothing like the way she actually looked.

And she *had* gained quite a bit of weight since those horrible, hungry days when she would often go more than two days without food.

"My name?" she asked, looking Jack squarely in the eye, her fear of what he might be thinking gone.

"Judith Bowen," she said, quickly inventing a false name. "My name is Judith Bowen." She pretended sadness by lowering her eyes. "My husband's name was . . . Timothy. My sweet daughter's was Priscilla."

She covered her face with her hands as she faked a deep, anguished sob behind them. "Lord, oh, Lord, I have lost everything," she cried. "My husband. My daughter! My . . . home!"

A rush of feet into the cabin made Speckled Fawn peek between her fingers. She saw a woman about the same size as she. Her face was pale, her hair wrapped in a tight chignon atop her head.

"Come on in, Darla Jane," Jack said.

"My, oh my," Darla Jane said as she rushed to Speckled Fawn with a dress hanging across her arm.

Moments after she arrived, another woman came into the cabin, carrying a basin of water.

"Jack, you and George can leave now," Darla Jane said, standing on tiptoe to brush a quick kiss across Jack's face. "Clara Belle and I will take care of the woman's needs. You go on and attend to your duties."

"Her name is Judith Bowen," Jack said over his shoulder as he and George turned and hurried to the door. "She's had a terrible experience. Help her, darlin', as you know how to help."

"I shall," Darla Jane said, then knelt down beside Speckled Fawn. "My dear, I am so sorry for your losses. But things will get better. I've seen it countless times since my husband joined the cavalry. Those awful Indians. Tsk, tsk. All savages. Every one of them redskins is a butchering savage. They should all be hanged for their crimes against humanity."

The woman's harsh opinion of Indians made it hard for Speckled Fawn to just lie there, listening to such condemnation of a people who had gotten a raw deal because of the greed and insensitivity of white leaders.

Speckled Fawn could hardly wait to leave this place, to be with her family of Indians again.

Just being there at the fort, with people who were so blind to the realities of life out West, was making her feel sick to her stomach.

Yes, she did see the Comanche renegades as savages, for they were responsible for terrible cruelty, and others with red skin were suffering the consequences of their attacks on settlers.

"I appreciate all of your kindnesses," Speckled Fawn forced herself to say as she slowly sat up on the bed.

She looked past the two women who were already there at a tiny, pretty, older woman who was just entering with an armload of bedding.

"What did you say your name was?" Darla Jane asked as she handed the dress to Speckled Fawn.

Speckled Fawn panicked, for she had forgotten her pretend name.

Then it came to her, and she heaved a deep sigh. "Judith," she said. "Judith Bowen."

"What a lovely name," the older woman said as she came and laid the linens on the bed beside Speckled Fawn. "Mine is Hannah. Hannah Cline. My husband is the colonel at this fort." She smiled. "Well, at least for now. I would hate to tell you how many different forts I have made my home in. Just as we get settled in, my Harold is sent somewhere else."

"It mustn't be the best way to live," Speckled Fawn said, trying to keep up her end of the conversation when all she really wanted was to be left alone until night drew its dark cloak over the fort. By then she hoped to have stolen little Megan away from her father and she could flee past the sentries at the front gate.

"I hope I'm allowed to stay until a riverboat comes that can take me back to civilization. I can't bear to stay in this wild and reckless land," Speckled Fawn said. She looked slowly from one woman to the next. "Do you think that is possible? Or am I going to be taken elsewhere, perhaps another fort?"

"My dear, a riverboat is expected very soon, and my husband will gladly pay your passage anywhere you wish to go," Hannah said, reaching down and gently shoving a fallen lock of hair back from Speckled Fawn's eyes. "All you have to do is name a city and your way will be paid to that destination."

"I cannot thank you enough for your kindness," Speckled Fawn said, taking Hannah's hand and gently holding it. "You are so very, very kind."

She clung to the hand, pretending it gave her a measure of comfort, as she again lowered her eyes and elaborated on her fictitious story. "I was alone in my cabin with my husband and child," she sobbed out. "Renegades came and killed my husband and daughter. They took me captive."

She looked slowly up at the women. "While the renegades slept, I . . . I . . . managed to escape," she said. "Somehow I managed to get to this fort. Thank the Lord, I was taken in. By the grace of God, I hope to begin a new life and put this all behind me. But it will be hard. I shall find it so hard to forget my husband and daughter's murder."

"We are so very sorry for all that you have been forced to endure," Hannah said, sighing heavily. "We've brought you clean clothes, bathwater, and we shall bring you food soon. Is there anything else you might want?"

"Yes, there is," Speckled Fawn said, her

pulse racing, for she knew her request was going to widen these women's eyes.

But she must ask, or her plan would never work.

"What is it, dear, and it is yours," Hannah said. She gently placed a hand on Speckled Fawn's cheek, although she visibly shuddered at touching such a dirty face.

"Could you please bring me a bottle of whiskey?" Speckled Fawn blurted out, amused to see how that suggestion affected the women.

Utterly shocked, the women gasped, almost in unison.

"You see," Speckled Fawn hurried on to say, "I'm not normally a drinker, but I need to find a way to help me forget what I witnessed. The blood . . . the screams."

The women turned pale and looked questioningly at each other.

"Truly, I don't know how else to erase the awful memories of my child and husband being slaughtered," Speckled Fawn said, wiping false tears. "Please understand I have been raised by the Bible's teachings and taught that alcohol is a sin. But at times like this—"

"We understand," Hannah said, interrupting Speckled Fawn. "Judith, if you feel that alcohol will help you sleep tonight, you shall have your whiskey. I can see how it might help." She smiled sheepishly. "I must admit that I sneak a tiny sip of whiskey from time to time, to help ease my qualms about some of the ungodly things my husband has been forced to do by his career. I shall bring you my own personal silver flask for you to sip from, but I would like the flask back in the morning."

Speckled Fawn was finding it amusing to see how shocked the two other women were by what Hannah had admitted about her drinking.

They continued to stare at her, their eyes wide, their faces now flushed rather than pale, at the knowledge that a woman of such high standing as Hannah Cline would drink such a foul thing as whiskey.

"I do thank you again for your kindness to me," Speckled Fawn said, then hung her head. "I would like to be alone now. I . . . I . . . would like to bathe, change my clothes, then rest."

She looked hurriedly up at Hannah. "Please bring the whiskey soon, for I am tormented by hideous visions, images that will haunt me for the rest of my life," she said, swallowing hard. "At least for tonight the whiskey can help erase such thoughts. Please bring it soon, Hannah. Please?"

"Wait and bathe after I get the whiskey, for I shall run and fetch it right now," Hannah said, turning and walking briskly to the door. She stopped and turned and looked at the women. "I believe I can trust you to keep my little secret to yourselves?"

The women nodded, assuring their silence.

"Thank you," Hannah murmured. "Now I think this woman needs her privacy, don't you?"

The women nodded and brushed past her;

then Hannah gave Speckled Fawn another smile over her shoulder and left as well.

Speckled Fawn laughed to herself, then knelt on the bed so she could gaze through the window at the cabin that she knew was occupied by Shirleen's husband. Its whereabouts had been explained carefully to her by the warrior who had followed Earl and his daughter earlier.

It was growing dark outside now, and she could see lamplight at the other cabin window.

She flinched when she saw a man silhouetted by the light. She knew it was Earl.

Then she felt her heart fill with love when she saw a child, and knew that she was looking at Shirleen's daughter.

"I will come for you soon, my darling," Speckled Fawn whispered, then felt the color drain from her face as she heard someone move up behind her in the cabin.

She turned, pale, and found herself gazing directly into Hannah Cline's eyes.

"What were you saying?" Hannah asked, holding a silver flask hidden beneath the end of her lacy shawl. "I am half deaf. Did you hear me come into the cabin? Were you saying something to me?"

A rush of relief flooded Speckled Fawn's senses. The words she had spoken to herself out loud had not been understood.

"I was saying a prayer," Speckled Fawn said, leaving the bed and standing beside Hannah. "I saw the first star of the evening shining brightly overhead. You know, the one that comes before total darkness falls."

"Yes, I know," Hannah said, slowly slipping the flask from beneath her shawl. "Here. Take it. But do not let any of the soldiers see it. My husband has no idea that I drink. A friend of mine steals the liquor from her husband's liquor cabinet and shares it with me."

Hannah giggled. "I have no idea how she explains the loss of the whiskey to her husband," she said. "Perhaps he accepts her pastime of drinking. Mine never would. He is too proud a man. He would never tolerate my doing something that he himself detests."

"I shall be very careful," Speckled Fawn said, taking the flask from Hannah. "I would never tell anyone who gave this to me. I just hope those two women who came with you will truly keep your secret."

"I am the wife of a powerful colonel. If those women know what's best for them and their husbands, they will keep their mouths shut," Hannah said tightly.

Then she quickly added. "Just don't you get caught."

"You can trust me," Speckled Fawn said. "Your secret is safe with me."

"I shall leave you now," Hannah said. "Food will be brought soon."

"Hannah, please don't bring me any food, or allow anyone else to," Speckled Fawn said. "My stomach would not tolerate food right now. I shall wait for breakfast, if that is alright with you."

"But whiskey should not be consumed on an empty stomach," Hannah protested.

"I know, but still, I just cannot even imagine eating now," Speckled Fawn said. "I . . . I . . . believe I would vomit the moment the food hit my stomach."

"I shall leave word that you do not want to dine with us tonight, nor do you want any supper brought to you here," Hannah said, placing a gentle hand on Speckled Fawn's face. "But please do be careful how much whiskey you consume on an empty stomach."

"I shall," Speckled Fawn promised. "I shall drink just what it takes to help lull me to sleep."

Hannah quickly hugged Speckled Fawn, then left, closing the door behind her.

"Whew," Speckled Fawn said, sighing heavily. "This is much harder than I imagined it would be."

She was not a practiced liar, but those lies were required in order for her to steal the child away.

She said a soft prayer that she would soon be with her husband again, and that Shirleen would be reunited with her daughter.

"I must succeed," she whispered as she held the flax out before her. "Yes, I must."

She gazed at the flask, then giggled. "If my dear mother could see me now," she murmured. "Oh, Mama. You would surely condemn me to hell if you knew what a sinner I can be."

But she did not really believe she was sinning tonight. She was thinking of anyone but herself!

Chapter Twenty-five

My heart aches, and a drowsy numbness pains
My sense, as though of hemlock I had drunk,
Or emptied some dull opiate to the drains.
                                    —Keats

Finally it was dark enough for Speckled Fawn to put her plan in motion. She felt it was safer for her to go to Earl's cabin after it got dark, hoping she wouldn't be seen. As she first stepped outside, she surveyed everything around her and saw that most inhabitants of the fort were inside their cabins.

She knew that at least one sentry would be keeping watch at the gate. She was hoping this sentry would fall asleep as the night wore on and she was ready to escape from the fort with Megan.

A lot of things had to fall into place or all would be lost for her. But for now the important thing was to be invited inside Earl's cabin, for she had the flask of whiskey hidden in her blouse as she stepped up to Earl's door.

She looked quickly around her. Seeing no one, she knocked.

Her heart pounded in her chest as she waited for the door to open. She knew he was still inside the cabin because she had slipped up to a window and taken a look before coming to the door.

She also knew that Megan was asleep on a small cot against the far wall.

The only other furniture in the cabin were a table and two chairs in the center of the room, as well as two comfortable-looking armchairs before a roaring fire.

She gathered that this was not a cabin used by a family but by a bachelor officer who used it primarily for sleeping. His meals were surely taken at the mess hall in the center of the courtyard.

Finally the door opened. Shirleen found herself looking into cold blue eyes as Earl stared glassily back at her. She saw how bloodshot his eyes were, and he reeked of alcohol. He must have already consumed a good amount of liquor.

She smiled to herself. The fact that he was already half drunk would help advance her plan that much more quickly.

"Why are you here?" Earl asked, his voice slurred. "As far as I can tell, there ain't nothin' here that should interest you."

"Your little girl," Speckled Fawn said, looking past him at the sleeping child. "I saw you earlier with the child. I . . . I . . . just recently lost my own daughter. Can I come in and see her? I am so lonesome for my baby."

"I heard about your tragedy," Earl said slyly, his blue eyes suddenly gleaming. He gestured with a hand. "Come on in. Take a gander at my little girl, if that will make your loss easier for you. But as you can see, my Megan's asleep. Don't wake her up."

"I won't," Speckled Fawn said, slipping past him before he had a chance to change his mind.

Hearing him speak Megan's name gave Speckled Fawn confirmation that this was the right child.

She went and stood over Megan, seeing how truly lovely she was, and how innocent. "I am so alone in the world now," she said, turning slowly to look at Earl, who came and stood behind her. "You seem alone, too. Can I stay for a while and talk?"

Earl slowly looked her up and down until he had gotten a full view of the buxom woman that she was. "Yeah, and how's about a drink with me?" he said, a wicked gleam in his eyes. "I'm lonely, too. Let's keep each other company for a while."

His eyes widened when Speckled Fawn slid the flask from beneath her blouse. "Well, what have we here?" he said, chuckling.

Speckled Fawn flinched when he grabbed the flask from her. "Come on," he said, drool spiraling from a corner of his mouth. "Sit. Drink." He winked at her. "Then maybe we can have ourselves some fun, if you know what I mean."

"Sir, I . . . just . . . lost my husband and

daughter," Speckled Fawn said, faking sadness. "But if you think it'd be alright, I would like to drink with you. That's why I brought the whiskey. I needed someone to drink with."

She frowned at him. "But that's all I want from you," she said firmly. "Company and booze. That's it. Do you understand?"

"That sounds good enough for me," Earl said, flopping down on a chair.

He motioned for her to sit down opposite him at the table. "Here," he said. "You brought the booze. You take the first drink from it. Go ahead. Take a swig."

He suddenly scooted the flask across the table to her.

Despising the very sight of the man, yet knowing she must proceed with the plan and then get out of there as quickly as she could, Speckled Fawn took the flask from him. She hadn't had a drink for many years and knew how quickly she could get drunk. She had to play it safe.

"Got a glass?" she asked, not wanting to share the taste of the man's mouth on the flask after he took a drink from it.

"Yep, think I can manage to find one," Earl said, stumbling out of his chair. He went to a small cabinet on the wall just above a table where a basin of water sat. He took two glasses from the cabinet, then went back and sat down on his chair opposite her.

He scooted one of the glasses over to her.

He watched with squinted eyes as she poured herself a small amount of whiskey.

"That's all you're gonna drink?" he asked, chuckling. "Just like a woman to brag about wantin' to drink, then you can't stand the taste of it. Go ahead. Drink what you like. I'll have no trouble drinkin' the rest."

Glad he assumed that most women hated whiskey, she smiled and took a sip.

He threw his head back in a fit of laughter. "That ain't enough to drown a fly in," he said as he took the flask back from her. "But it just leaves more for me."

When the whiskey hit Speckled Fawn's belly, she cringed. This had to be the worst liquor she had ever tasted. And she knew it was very strong.

She was glad that Earl wasn't pushing any more on her. She would just take delight in watching him get drunker and drunker, and then take advantage of him when she could.

She watched him down one glass of whiskey and then another. He became quiet, seeming more interested in getting drunk than anything else.

"Whiskey helps a lot when you need to forget," he said, his words slurring even more than before. "I need to forget. Oh, Lordie, if you only knew what I seen recently. Well, you don't want to know, and I cain't ever say."

Speckled Fawn knew what he wanted to forget without his telling her, so she just stayed quiet and waited for him to pass out.

He was having trouble keeping his head up, and each time he took another drink, much of the whiskey sloshed out of the glass onto his lips.

He was losing control.

That was what Speckled Fawn wanted.

She had worked in enough dance halls to recognize the signs before a man passed out.

Thank the Lord, this man was nearing that point now.

"I was wrong to take my daughter from her mother," Earl suddenly blurted out.

He looked over at Megan, who was still sleeping soundly. "I do regret taking the child to raise by myself," he said. "I only took her to bring hurt into my wife's heart. I've grown tired of her and the child. And now here I am, stuck with a child to raise all by myself."

His words were so slurred Speckled Fawn could hardly make out what he was saying. But knowing so much about him from what Shirleen had told her, she could decipher enough of what he was saying to make sense of it.

He slid a slow gaze over at Speckled Fawn. His eyes glittered glassily. "Since you've lost your own daughter, would you like to have mine to take her place?" he asked thickly. "I'd gladly part with her. She's done what I needed her for. Now I'd like a life of my own, alone."

Speckled Fawn was stunned by the way things were happening. Never had she expected this. She realized now just how evil-hearted this man was.

"If you don't truly want her, why did you take her?" she asked cautiously.

"Don't you hear well? Have you got cotton or something else in your ears?" he said, squinting at her again. "I told you I took Megan in order to hurt her mother."

He leaned closer to Speckled Fawn. "I'm serious," he said. "Would you like to have the child? Yours was taken from you by the heathens. Now you can have mine instead. Take my daughter and you'll no longer be alone."

He chuckled again and began talking even more erratically. "How'd you escape your captors?" he said. "You're mighty clever to have done it."

He didn't give her a chance to answer because he didn't really want an answer. He just wanted to ramble on and on. "I hate all redskins," he said, glowering. "They are murdering, lice-infested savages." He chuckled as he stared at the flask of whiskey. "I had me an Indian squaw one day. It was about a year ago. I'd been out alone hunting and there she was, all alone, picking berries. I recognized her. She was known to be the wife of a powerful Assiniboine Indian chief. She was Chief Blue Thunder's woman."

Afraid of what else this man was going to tell her, Speckled Fawn felt sick even before he confirmed her suspicion. She was almost sure that she was sitting face-to-face with the son of a bitch who had ended the life of her chief's wife.

But Speckled Fawn had to play his game. She knew he enjoyed telling her what he had done. He deserved what he would eventually get. A man like him wouldn't live long. Someone would take offense at his arrogance and silence him forever.

"I've not heard of that Indian chief," she lied. "Or his wife."

"Well, you're hearing about her now," he said, snickering. "I threw that squaw to the ground. My, oh my, did she plead and fight as I raped her. When I was done, I silenced her forever with my knife."

Speckled Fawn tried not to show how horrified she was feeling. Oh, Lord, she was face-to-face with a rapist and murderer.

She flinched when Earl suddenly slapped the knife sheathed at his right side.

"This here is the knife that did it," he bragged. "There's one less savage squaw on this earth now because of me. I believe the Comanche renegades were accused of the crime, for no one ever came lookin' for good ol' Earl Mingus."

He leaned even close to her. "See?" he said. "I did you a favor. The Comanche came and killed your husband and child, didn't they?"

"Yes, Comanche, but not Assiniboine," she dared to say. "They are known to be peace-loving people."

He frowned. "Are you an Injun lover or what?" he said, his head swaying as the alcohol fully claimed him.

"No, you must know I'm not, after suffering such losses because of them," she said. She rose from the chair and went to Megan. She looked over her shoulder at Earl, whose head was resting on the table. "Are you serious? Can I truly have the child? I promise to be a good mother."

He shrugged. "That doesn't matter. I just wanna get her outta my hair," he said. "Take her."

He lifted his head unsteadily from the table and gazed at Speckled Fawn through blurred vision. "But where will you take her?" he said. "Your home was burned."

"I have a friend who lives in a small settlement not far from where my cabin had been," she said, hoping that her lie was believable. "Until the child is older and better able to travel, I'll stay there. Then later I will head for Boston, my true home. Don't you agree with me that the long journey back East would be too hard on the child if I took her there now?"

"Probably so," he said, shrugging.

"Then you agree to my plan?" she asked. "Can I truly take her? Take her now?"

He nodded and stood shakily. Then he watched Speckled Fawn gather Megan up from the bed and into her arms. The child slept through it all.

"Thank you," Speckled Fawn said as she glanced quickly at Earl, then rushed out of the cabin.

She was glad there was no moon.

Everything was pitch-black as she headed toward the gate.

She looked over her shoulder at the cabins. She saw no lamplight in any of them. Everyone else had gone to bed for the night.

She prayed that the sentry was asleep, too.

She also prayed that the gate could be easily opened without making noise.

Breathlessly she made her way toward the gate, disbelieving her luck. She had a feeling that when tomorrow came, and Earl was sober and realized what he had done, he would decide to come after Megan.

The good thing was, he would have no idea where to look. By then, Megan would be safely in her mother's arms.

Speckled Fawn was certain that God was with her tonight, because she found the gate ajar and the sentry fast asleep.

She prayed that the child wouldn't wake up at the wrong time.

She slowly stepped outside, past the sentry.

Then she held Megan near to her heart and ran as fast as she could until she fell into Blue Thunder's arms. He gently took the child, who awakened at that moment, her eyes wide with fear when she found she was in the company of Indians.

"You are safe with us," Blue Thunder tried to reassure her. "You are going to be alright. I am taking you to your mother."

Megan's eyes widened; then she trustingly

hugged Blue Thunder. He took her to his horse and mounted, holding her carefully on his lap.

With pride in her eyes, Speckled Fawn rode beside Blue Thunder as they headed back toward the village. Now she would be fully accepted by Blue Thunder. She had finally proved her worth to him.

She could hardly wait to get home and tell her husband what she had done, although she knew that he probably wouldn't be able to hear her in his deep sleep.

She hoped a miracle would happen and he would awaken again as he had before.

Chapter Twenty-six

Kiss the tears from her eyes,
You'll find the rose
The sweeter for the dew.

—Webster

Shirleen was stirred from her sleep by the
sound of horses outside.

Was she dreaming?

Or was she truly hearing horses coming into
the village?

Having remained fully dressed as she had
stretched out before the night's fire, she
rushed to her feet and ran outside. She could
see Blue Thunder's face beneath the moon's
glow, and then, oh, Lord, she saw her sweet
Megan lying nestled on Blue Thunder's lap,
asleep.

Shirleen was overwhelmed with a joy she
had never known possible as she ran toward
the oncoming horses, her arms outstretched.

When Blue Thunder saw her, he drew rein
and dismounted, handing Megan to her. Only
then did the child awaken and realize what
was happening.

"Mama! Mama!" Megan cried, clinging to Shirleen's neck. "Oh, Mama, Papa took me away! I didn't want to go, but he took me anyway!"

"I know, dear," Shirleen said, gazing lovingly at her daughter, wondering if this was real or if she was dreaming.

But her daughter's arms around her neck were real enough!

Her tiny body cuddled so close to Shirleen's was real!

Shirleen looked through thankful tears at Blue Thunder as he stood there, smiling, watching the wondrous reunion of *ina* and *micinski*.

Then he suddenly became aware of the silence around him as the people of the village came out of their lodges, solemnly staring at him.

He looked at one person and then another. Finally he noticed someone standing at the doorway of his uncle's lodge.

His people's shaman, Morning Thunder.

He also realized that when he had first seen Shirleen, she had come from his own lodge, not his uncle's, where she had promised to stay until he returned with his uncle's wife.

Speckled Fawn also became aware that things were not as they should be. She could feel the color draining from her face when she, too, saw Morning Thunder standing just outside her husband's lodge.

She looked quickly at Shirleen, who had

promised to stay with Dancing Shadow while Speckled Fawn went to help rescue the younger woman's child.

She gazed into Shirleen's eyes. "What has happened?" Speckled Fawn asked in a faint whisper, for she was almost certain of the answer without hearing it.

"I am so sorry," Shirleen said softly.

"He . . . is . . . dead?" Speckled Fawn cried out as she slid from her saddle. "My husband . . . ?"

"He died peacefully with a smile on his face, for he thought I was you," Shirleen said, her voice catching. "He . . . even . . . spoke some last words to me, and they were about you, Speckled Fawn. Only you."

"And I wasn't there," Speckled Fawn choked out. With tears streaming from her eyes, she broke into a run and was soon inside her lodge, at her husband's side.

Shirleen turned to Blue Thunder. "I truly did all that I could," she said, a sob catching in her throat. "I talked with him those few moments when he finally found voice enough to speak. He . . . did . . . seem content to die."

"He was always a contented man, so it would not be different when he knew that he was on his way to the stars and beyond," Blue Thunder said. He stepped over to Shirleen and wrapped his comforting arms around both her and Megan. "He had done all that he could for his people, and he knew that. He also had found great contentment in finally having a wife."

"I am so glad that he found such happiness on this earth," Shirleen murmured. "So few have that opportunity."

"I have found much happiness myself, caring for my people," Blue Thunder said thickly. "And that happiness has become twofold since meeting you. Now I can share more happiness with you, since I know yours is more complete because you have your daughter with you again."

"I can hardly believe she is here," Shirleen said. Megan had fallen asleep again, but this time against her bosom, not Blue Thunder's.

"Let us take her where she can rest comfortably," Blue Thunder said, slipping gently away from Shirleen. "I will tell you all about her rescue, and then I must go and sit with my uncle."

With Blue Thunder's arm around Shirleen's waist, they walked toward their tepee, leaving their horses to be tended by the young brave who remained dutiful to his chief's wishes. Around them, families were reunited and speaking softly of the death that had come into their village, as well as a new life.

After Megan was resting comfortably on a bed of pelts, Shirleen and Blue Thunder knelt together awhile beside the sleeping child.

They each kissed Megan's brow, and then went to sit beside the lodge fire.

After Blue Thunder added wood to the fire and the flames were leaping upward, sending warmth and light throughout the tepee,

Shirleen and Blue Thunder sat down on a thick pallet of furs, and he told her in depth how the rescue had transpired.

"And so Earl actually stole our daughter away only to spite me, not out of love for Megan," Shirleen said, anger like a hot poker inside her belly. "He did not concern himself for one minute how the child was feeling. He only thought of himself, as always. He is perhaps the cruelest man that walks the earth."

"Just be thankful that Speckled Fawn was able to get Megan away from Earl so easily, and that she succeeded in leaving the fort without being seen," Blue Thunder said soothingly. "All else is no longer important."

"Tell me all of it," Shirleen said, moving to her knees in front of Blue Thunder, her eyes searching his. "Tell me everything."

He reached out and gently touched her face, then proceeded to tell her all that she was eager to hear.

And when he was finished, she was awed by Speckled Fawn's daring, but mainly so happy that everything had worked out and her daughter was with her now, forever.

"Your Megan is quite wonderful," Blue Thunder said. He reached out and drew Shirleen onto his lap. She twined an arm around his neck and nestled close to him. "As are you, my woman."

"You have no idea how happy I am at this moment," Shirleen said, then leaned away from him and gazed into his eyes. "Yet so *sad*. I could feel Speckled Fawn's grief when she realized her husband was dead. I could feel the sadness of your people."

"It is sad in one respect, good in another," Blue Thunder said. He twined his fingers through her thick red hair, pushing it back from her face and draping it over her shoulders. "My uncle has been only half a man now for so long. He is whole again as he walks the road to the hereafter with those who went ahead of him. He is a full man again, in all respects. When he laughs, he realizes that he is laughing. When he speaks, his words are true and from the heart. And when he gazes down from the heavens to see his wife, he knows that she mourns for him, but knows, too, that she feels him with her now, as if he were sitting with her, holding her hand. You see, my woman, his body no longer functions, but his spirit is very much alive."

"That is so beautifully put," Shirleen murmured, more and more in awe of this man the longer she knew him.

She was so blessed that he would soon be her husband.

He would be her daughter's father!

"I must go now and sit with my uncle alongside Speckled Fawn for a while," he said thickly. "We will take but one day to mourn his death. He has been ready to go and join his loved ones among the stars for a long time."

He took Shirleen's hands and looked into her eyes. "In truth, his passing is a joyous time for me, as well as sad. It was painful to see my uncle so different from the way he used to be, a strong and vital person . . . a beloved shaman."

He framed Shirleen's face between his hands. "My woman, I feel deeply for my uncle's wife, for if I did not know earlier, I do know now how much she loved him and is truly grieving his passing," he said, his voice hoarse with emotion.

"Yes, she did love him so much," Shirleen said softly. "I could tell by the way she talked about him to me. Were he young and more vital, she could not have loved him any more than she did."

"Soon, my love, soon we shall join hands and hearts as husband and wife," Blue Thunder said. He gently lifted her off his lap. "I shall make certain no harm befalls you or your child ever again. I will protect you, my woman, with my life."

Shirleen flung her arms around his neck and met his lips with her own. Their kiss was all-consuming, and then he was gone from the tepee, leaving her alone with her child.

Tears flowed from her eyes—joyous tears at the thought that she and her daughter had found a new life. They would be safe and happy among these beautiful people, and especially with Blue Thunder.

Going to kneel beside Megan, Shirleen gently

touched her cheek, then bent low and kissed her tiny lips. "Sweet thing, you are with your mommy now, and I promise you that no one will ever harm you again . . . especially not your evil papa!"

Chapter Twenty-seven

Quick!
I wait!
And who can tell what tomorrow may befall.
Love me more, or not at all.
—Sill

Lurid flashes of lightning could be seen through the smoke hole. Loud rumbles of thunder ensued as Blue Thunder sat beside Speckled Fawn and they gazed at their lifeless loved one.

Speckled Fawn fought back tears. She had already shed so many as she sat with Blue Thunder in silence, both grieving the passing of a wonderful man.

Yet Speckled Fawn could not keep her thoughts completely focused on her departed husband. She kept hearing the horrible words that Earl had spoken . . . about how he had raped, then killed Blue Thunder's wife!

The day Shawnta's body had been found was one of pure horror. She had been brutally raped, then stabbed to death.

When she had been brought back into the village in her husband's arms, it seemed that the world stopped dead still at that moment. The whole Wind Band had come from their lodges to see their fallen loved one, and to witness her terrible death.

Mourning had been sudden and intense. It had lasted for days upon days until Blue Thunder had finally given up his wife to the spirits.

But although she was in the ground, Blue Thunder had still not given her up completely. He had sat at that gravesite for hours at a time, usually only coming home to sleep.

He had not eaten during that time of grieving, nor had he performed his chieftain's duties, which had been carried out by his most trusted warriors.

After he finally accepted his loss, he had spent days, weeks, even months, searching for the one who had killed his wife.

But no matter how far he rode with his warriors, searching for anyone who might know of a man who would be so evil as to ambush a lone woman and defile her body in such a way, no one knew the answers to his questions.

It was only recently that people had begun to whisper that Big Nose and his renegades were responsible. Yet Big Nose was elusive, seemingly impossible to capture.

Unable to hold inside herself what she knew any longer, Speckled Fawn reached a hand over and placed it on Blue Thunder's arm, drawing his questioning gaze to her.

"My chief, I have something to tell you," she said in a whisper.

Another flash of lightning lit up the buffalo covering of the tepee, and the following thunder shook the ground beneath them.

Blue Thunder looked at her askance, for this was not the time for small talk. He turned away from her, wondering what could be so important that she would speak up at such a time as this.

Yet he would not ask her. His respect for his uncle was too great to speak in his presence, although Dancing Shadow would never hear anyone again.

"Blue Thunder . . ." Speckled Fawn said persistently. "Please come outside with me. I have something that must be said."

Blue Thunder frowned at her, then seeing something in her eyes, and hearing the insistence in her voice, he rose and stood over her as she pushed herself up from the mat-covered floor.

They walked outside, where the skies were dark and the lightning and thunder continued.

The first raindrop fell, and then two, and another and another from the savage skies above.

"Hurry and say what you must say," Blue Thunder urged. He gazed up at the sky. He had never seen it look so threatening before.

He flinched when lightning zigzagged from one cloud to another, the ensuing thunder even more pronounced this time.

"Oh, Blue Thunder, I know you need to know what I have learned, yet I find it so hard to tell you," Speckled Fawn said, her voice catching.

She lowered her eyes for a moment, to gather the courage to tell him the truth.

Blue Thunder was stunned to see Speckled Fawn actually having trouble saying something. He had never known a woman who loved to talk so much.

She was so loquacious, sometimes she got on his nerves!

"Just tell me," he said, taking her elbow and guiding her toward his tepee when the raindrops came in a rush from the heavens.

When Speckled Fawn saw where Blue Thunder was taking her, she grabbed his arm and led him in a different direction. She did not want to tell him about Earl in front of Shirleen.

She knew Shirleen would have to hear what Earl had done, but Blue Thunder deserved privacy when he learned the awful truth.

She led him into the small tepee that had housed Shirleen upon her first arrival at the village. Although it was dark inside because no fire burned in the fire pit, the continued flashes of lightning provided enough light to see each other.

"I have never seen you behave so strangely," Blue Thunder said, wiping Speckled Fawn's face dry with the palms of his hands.

He wiped his own face dry, then lifted his wet hair back over his shoulders as he awaited some sort of response from Speckled Fawn besides a strange stare.

"It will be so hard to say," Speckled Fawn murmured. "But oh, Blue Thunder, I must."

Growing impatient, Blue Thunder placed his hands on her shoulders and looked intently into her eyes. "Say it," he said tightly. "Say . . . it . . . now."

Although he was urging her to tell him whatever it was she found so hard to say, he was now dreading her next words.

And something else was troubling him besides her behavior. The storm had worsened, bringing heavy sheets of rain. The air was heavy. The winds were howling, bringing gusts of rain down through the smoke hole.

He was sorry to realize that this rain could delay his uncle's burial, for the burial grounds would be too muddy. He had wanted to get the burial behind him so that he could know his uncle's spirit would be free.

"My chief, it was not renegades who took your wife from you," Speckled Fawn finally blurted out. "It was not renegades who . . . defiled . . . her body so horribly."

Blue Thunder was taken aback by what she was saying. His heart seemed misplaced inside his chest. It seemed to be everywhere at once, pounding, pounding, pounding!

"How would you know this?" he finally managed to ask.

His grip on her shoulders tightened so much she winced.

He saw what he had done and drew his hands quickly away.

"While I was at the fort, talking with Shirleen's husband, much was revealed to me that had nothing to do with Shirleen," Speckled Fawn said.

"What was revealed?" Blue Thunder demanded, his jaw tight, for he was becoming more and more annoyed by all the delays.

"Shirleen's husband, Earl Mingus, was the one responsible for your wife's death, not Big Nose and his Comanche renegades," Speckled Fawn finally found the courage to say.

Blue Thunder felt as though someone had struck him. The news that Speckled Fawn had just told him was so shocking, it seemed unreal.

"How would you know this?" he finally managed to ask, his voice drawn.

"Because he told me," Speckled Fawn said solemnly. "He had consumed quite a bit of whiskey even before I arrived at his cabin. After he drank more of what I brought, his tongue was loosened. He bragged about things that he had done, mainly finding a lovely Indian maiden in the forest, alone, and . . . and . . . raping and killing her."

Blue Thunder felt himself grow dizzy as he heard this horrible truth. Yet when it had sunk in, he became strong in mind and body again.

He doubled his hands into tight fists at his sides. "Tell me all that he told you," he said thickly. "Leave nothing out, not even something you might think would hurt me too much to hear. Remember that I am strong in all ways. I am strong enough to hear the worst."

His heart pounded hard in his chest as Speckled Fawn told him about everything Earl had said, and how the man was so proud to have raped and killed an Indian woman.

Nothing in Blue Thunder's lifetime had been as devastating to hear as what Speckled Fawn had just told him.

He hungered now for vengeance against this man who was not even truly a man, but a gutless, cowardly animal.

He could finally avenge the terrible wrongs that had been done to his beloved wife.

To remember her was to remember sweetness, the sort of sweetness that he had found again in the woman he would soon marry.

To take such sweetness from this earth was the worst possible crime a man could commit, in Blue Thunder's opinion.

"What are you going to do?" Speckled Fawn asked guardedly as she saw the rage in her chief's eyes. "And when? The riverboat should be arriving soon. Earl plans to be on it."

Then she gazed out the entrance flap at the torrential rain falling from the sky.

She turned toward Blue Thunder again. "Yet I doubt now that the boat will be arriving, or leaving, anytime soon," she said, slowly smiling. "You see, I know riverboats and the habits of their captains. During my years of being alone, fleeing from one town to another, I spent many an hour hidden on riverboats. When the weather is as bad as it is today, the rivers rise too much for the boats to travel. The captains find a safe place to tie up, then wait out the storm. This will give you enough time to stop Earl Mingus before he boards the paddlewheeler."

Blue Thunder gazed with grateful eyes at Speckled Fawn. He reached a hand out and placed it gently on her face. "During your time in my village I have not treated you as well as I should have," he said quietly. "You see, I never understood why my uncle preferred a white woman over one of his own skin color, but now I think I know why he wanted you as his wife. He saw in you what I couldn't, or should I say, refused to. That proves just how wise a man my uncle was, for there could not have been any better wife than you were to him."

Deeply touched by what he'd said, Speckled Fawn flung herself into his arms, sobbing. Their wet clothes clung as they hugged.

Then, wiping her eyes with the backs of her hands, Speckled Fawn stepped away from him. "Are you going to tell Shirleen what I just told you?" she asked softly.

"Every word," Blue Thunder said flatly. "She already knows how evil Earl Mingus is, and now she shall know just how fortunate she is to no longer be with this man. I will also tell her that when I avenge my wife's death by killing him, I shall also take revenge for the beatings she received. He will pay for each of the scars that he inflicted on her back!"

He walked past Speckled Fawn and held the flap aside as he gazed up at the black sky.

There was no letup.

The lightning continued to flash. The thunder and the wind continued to roar.

He gave Speckled Fawn a smile over his shoulder, thanked her for being who she was, then ran out into the cold rain.

He had promised Shirleen that he would protect her forever.

Now he was even more determined to do so, for he knew there were countless men, both white and red-skinned, who were as evil as Earl Mingus.

But Earl just might be the worst of them all.

Chapter Twenty-eight

To nestle once more in
That haven of rest—
Your lips upon mine,
My head on your breast.

—Hunt

His hair dripping wet, Blue Thunder ran into his tepee, stopping quickly when he found Shirleen pacing, her eyes wild with fear.

He hurried to her, and forgetting how wet his clothes were, he took her into his arms and hugged her close to him.

"I . . . am . . . so afraid of storms," Shirleen sobbed, clinging to Blue Thunder as she trembled against his powerful body.

She was so gripped by her fear, she did not even notice that his clothes were wetting her own.

"I am here," Blue Thunder said, gently stroking her back. "You are safe from all harm."

"I wasn't when I lived with Earl," she said, finally composing herself. She still clung to Blue Thunder even when she realized her clothes were becoming as wet as his.

But that didn't matter.

The fact that he was there with her, protecting her as no man had since she had left the protective home of her father and mother, was all that mattered.

"He is someone you need not think about again, or fear," Blue Thunder said softly. "He will never come near you again."

"But it will still be hard to forget the terrible memories that are evoked by thunder and lightning. I am afraid I shall always associate storms with . . . with . . . Earl Mingus," she said, vividly recalling Earl's bizarre behavior during the most violent storms.

"Why is that?" Blue Thunder asked, stepping away from her. He gazed questioningly into her eyes, which were red from crying. "What has he to do with storms?"

He looked past her at the sleeping child. He found it strange that Megan would be sleeping through the horrible booms of thunder, which shook the ground upon which she slept, while her mother was so afraid of them.

Feeling much more at ease now that Blue Thunder was there with his wonderful way of soothing her woes, Shirleen was able to take a deep breath. Then she became aware of Blue Thunder gazing at Megan.

She turned and looked at her daughter, too. "She sleeps so soundly," she murmured. "The experience she has just gone through has exhausted her. She woke for a minute when the storm began, but I took her into my arms and rocked her until she fell asleep."

"She will be alright," Blue Thunder said, trying to reassure Shirleen of something he was not sure of himself.

But they both had to believe that in time Megan would be able to leave behind the dreadfulness of these past days, now that she was no longer the prisoner of a father who used her as a pawn.

"Yes, I know," Shirleen murmured. She wiped away fresh tears from her eyes, then turned and looked at Blue Thunder standing there dripping wet. "You will catch your death of cold if you don't get out of those clothes. Let me help you."

In a matter of moments his wet clothes were removed and he wore fresh buckskins.

Shirleen dried his hair with a soft cloth. Then they stood before one another, their gazes meeting and holding.

He noticed how she flinched when the thunder boomed again, and how her eyes took on a frightened look.

"Tell me what he did to you while it stormed to make you dread thunder and lightning so much," he said. He took her hand and led her down onto the plush pelts beside the warm fire. "Once you release the memory from inside you by telling me about it, you will be rid of it forever. I will see that thoughts of that evil man never come into your mind or heart again when it storms."

"He was . . . is . . . such a maniac," Shirleen said. She nervously pushed her thick hair back from her face as she gazed into the dancing flames of the fire.

Then she looked quickly over at Blue Thunder. "Earl loved storms," she explained. "He would go outside during the worst of a storm. He would stand there laughing hysterically as he gazed up at the sky. It was as though the demon in him was unleashed during storms."

She lowered her eyes, swallowed hard, then gazed into Blue Thunder's eyes. "After the storm passed over, Earl would come back inside our home and throw me to the floor and force himself on me sexually. It didn't matter if Megan was standing there, witnessing this cruelty to her mother. She saw me wince and cry out as Earl became like a wild man when he finally reached sexual release."

She paused, gazed over her shoulder to be certain that Megan was asleep, then looked into Blue Thunder's eyes, again. "Once he was finished with me, he would give me a kick, then leave the house for a long time," she said coldly. "He . . . would . . . go away on his horse for hours at a time. I never knew what he was doing, or where he was going. I was just glad that he was finally gone so that I could compose myself and . . . and . . . try to help Megan get the horrible sight of what had happened to her mother out of her mind by telling her stories and singing to her."

The more Shirleen told about how horribly

treated she had been by that maniac, the more
determined Blue Thunder was to prevent Earl
Mingus from boarding the riverboat. Blue
Thunder was going to make certain Earl could
never abuse another woman as he had abused
not only his beloved Shirleen, but also his precious former wife.

As the thunder continued to roar and the
lightning raced across the heavens, sending its
bright flashes through the buffalo covering of
the tepee, Blue Thunder reached for Shirleen.
He brought her over to sit on his lap, facing
him.

"I have something to tell you," he said thickly
as she searched his eyes with her own. "I was
not sure if I should tell you just yet about it,
but after hearing what that crazed white man
did to you, I feel this is the exact time that I
should tell you something about Earl . . .
and . . . my wife."

"Earl and your wife?" Shirleen said, her eyes
widening in wonder. "What is there to say?"

"While Speckled Fawn was drinking with
Earl, he bragged about something that horrified her," he said angrily. "It is so horrible I
cannot rest until vengeance is mine. And it
shall be, soon."

"What did Speckled Fawn tell you?" Shirleen
asked, almost afraid to hear the answer.

"That hideous man bragged to Speckled
Fawn that he raped and killed an Indian
woman . . . who was my wife," Blue Thunder
said, his voice revealing a mixture of

emotions—hate, sadness, and, yes, a deep need for vengeance.

"What?" Shirleen gasped, clutching her throat. "He told her . . . what?"

Both thought of Megan at the same time and turned to look at her before saying anything else about the horrors Earl had committed.

When they found that she was still sleeping soundly, a blanket drawn up to her chin, they looked into each other's eyes again.

He repeated what Speckled Fawn had told him, how the rape had occurred, and then the murder.

"Lord, oh, Lord," Shirleen said. "I knew he had a sadistic side, but I didn't know he could be so completely evil."

"You are fortunate you were not harmed worse than the beatings, my woman," Blue Thunder said, twining his arms around her and drawing her against his chest. "It could have been you. He could have killed you, too, with the same knife that he used on my wife."

Suddenly a memory came to Shirleen that caused her to jerk quickly away from Blue Thunder. She swallowed hard as she gazed intently into his eyes.

"There was a day, about a year ago, when Earl came home from a hunt empty-handed and with a look of sadistic glee on his face that made me shudder," Shirleen said, even now cold inside at the memory. "When I asked him about what happened while he was gone, why there was blood on his clothes even though he had caught nothing, he just laughed at me and said, 'Wouldn't you like to know?'"

She swallowed hard again. "That must have been the day he raped and killed your wife, for Earl didn't touch me that night, which was unusual. Normally he never let me go to sleep without forcing me to do my wifely duty. He was a man with a never-ending appetite for sex. But that day? He seemed so pleased with himself, he did not need what he usually demanded from me."

"When I am through with him, he will never again take sadistic pleasure from a helpless woman," Blue Thunder said tightly.

"When will you go after him?" Shirleen asked.

"Soon," he said, then eased her from his lap and placed her next to him. He reached for a blanket and brought it around both their shoulders. "As soon as the storm ends, my warriors and I will set out to find him. He will regret all of the wrongs that he has done to so many."

He purposely changed the subject. "As soon as the ground is ready to receive my uncle, we will bury him," he said softly. "But since the ground will not be ready for two sleeps, I will leave and take care of that other matter in the meantime."

"I feel so blessed to have had those last moments with your uncle," Shirleen said, recalling how Dancing Shadow had spoken to her and smiled. For a moment she had thought he was improving, whereas in truth he was moments away from taking his last breath. "I discovered during those moments why everyone loved him so much."

"He will be missed," Blue Thunder said. "But he had a full life. He helped so many of our people when he was our shaman. He will never be forgotten."

He turned to her and smiled into her eyes. "And soon everyone will see how much I love you, for there will be a wedding at the first opportunity," he said, then drew her against him and gave her a sweet kiss.

He wanted Shirleen with every fiber of his being tonight, but for now, he would just relish these moments with her and her daughter.

But soon they would be man and wife and would hold each other and make sweet love each and every night.

He hoped they would bring a brother or sister into the world for Megan to love and adore. But whether that happened or not, she would no longer be an only child, for she would have Little Bee as her sister.

There would be much laughter around their lodge fire on cold winter nights. There would be popped corn passed around to brothers and sisters, for that was a special treat that Blue Thunder had shared with friends because he had no brother or sister to share it with.

He smiled at the thought of their future together, when all ugliness and sadness was finally a thing of the past!

But tomorrow?

He would ride from the village with vengeance like hot coals inside his belly. He would not rest until he knew that Earl Mingus no longer drew breath.

"I feel much better about the storm now that you are with me," Shirleen said.

"Storms pass, but other things of the heavens never die," Blue Thunder said, hoping to distract her from her fear of the storm. He gazed into her eyes. "Have you ever been intrigued by stars?"

"Always," she murmured. "I have spent many hours staring up at the night sky, oh, so mystified by the moon and stars."

"You are aware of what is called the Milky Way by your people?" Blue Thunder asked, smiling into her eyes.

"Yes, I have often looked at it in wonder," she said, remembering those nights when she had sat on her father's lap on their front porch as he rocked her in the white wicker rocking chair.

"My people call it *moch-pe-achan-ka-hoo*, the backbone of the sky," Blue Thunder said. "We believe it is as necessary to the support of the heavens as the backbone of any animal to its body."

"That is a beautiful way to think about it," Shirleen said. "My father would have loved that description of the Milky Way."

"Would you like to hear what my people think about the moon?" Blue Thunder said. "It is not believed to influence men or plants, nor to have any other property except to give light by night. My people believe the moon is eaten up by a number of moles, and Wakonda makes a new one upon the destruction of the old moon."

He placed his hands at her waist and lifted her to sit on his lap, facing him. "My woman, I know you feel sad about my uncle's death, but where he will live upon his spirit's arrival in the heavens is a place much better than any upon this earth. It is an Indian paradise, where there is perpetual summer, abundance of grass, beautiful women, and every comfort Dancing Shadow might ever wish for. Also, he will see his friends and relatives. No quarrels, wars, or bodily pain exist there. All live in perfect harmony. So we should not mourn his departure from this earth, but rejoice in his going to a better place."

"I am a religious person and attended church regularly with my parents before I left home with Earl, but no preacher ever spoke so beautifully of heaven," she murmured.

"That is because your heaven and the Assiniboine's are vastly different," Blue Thunder said softly.

"Then which Heaven will I go to once I become your wife?" she asked.

"My people's because that is where I will one day go, and we shall never part once we have joined our hearts as husband and wife," Blue Thunder said. He smiled as she flung herself into his arms and gave him a wonderful hug, making it clear that she did not want to part from him ever, even in death.

He now knew that he had definitely chosen the right woman to be his wife.

"My woman, I have something for you," he suddenly said. He had not planned to give her the special gift just yet. He had thought to present her with this gift on their wedding day, but she had gone through so much of late, perhaps the gift would make her feel loved and appreciated even more than his words of encouragement.

"A gift?" Shirleen said as he gently lifted her from his lap. He took her hand and encouraged her to stand.

She turned and watched him go to one of his buckskin bags in which he stored his personal belongings.

When she saw what he took from it, her eyes widened. The fire's glow revealed a necklace that Blue Thunder now held spread out between his hands as he came back and stood before her.

She could not take her eyes off it as the silver reflected the shine of the lodge fire. The silver was adorned with many dazzling turquoise settings in the shape of teardrops.

"This was my grandmother's necklace, but never worn by her," Blue Thunder said thickly. "My grandfather had it made for his wife, to present to her as a special gift. The day before he had planned to give it to her, she died."

"How . . . sad . . ." Shirleen stammered.

"My grandfather gave it to me to present to the woman I chose to marry," Blue Thunder said.

"Then it was . . . your . . . wife's?" Shirleen asked, gazing into his dark eyes.

"My wife had already died," Blue Thunder said softly. "My grandfather encouraged me to take another wife soon, not pine away for the one I had lost. My grandfather said that the necklace should be worn by that wife."

"It is so beautiful," Shirleen murmured, again looking at it and truly loving it.

"My grandfather was a wise man," he said. "He was right to encourage me to take another wife. He has joined his wife in the heavens, but I wish he was here to see the one I have chosen to be my bride. He would have smiled at my choice."

"Even though I am white?" Shirleen asked, searching his eyes.

"It is not always the color of one's skin that is important," Blue Thunder said, stepping behind her and fastening the necklace in place. "It is one's heart that matters the most, and, my woman, yours is a good and caring heart. You will make the perfect wife for this Assiniboine chief."

Touched to the very core of her being, Shirleen reached up and placed her fingers on the necklace that now hung so beautifully around her neck. Blue Thunder came around and stood before her to admire it.

He gently touched her cheek. "It is rightfully

yours," he said thickly. "A beautiful necklace for a beautiful woman."

"I shall proudly wear it," Shirleen said, smiling into his eyes. "When you are called away from our home for some reason, the necklace will make me feel as though you are still with me."

Their lips met in a long, sweet kiss.

"I love you so," she whispered against his mouth.

Chapter Twenty-nine

And I will make thee a bed of roses,
And a thousand fragrant posies.

—Marlowe

Blue Thunder awakened with a start when a voice spoke from outside his tepee.

He looked at Shirleen and saw that she still slept, so he rose as quietly as possible from their bed of blankets and pelts.

He had worn a breechclout to bed so he was able to go directly to the entrance flap, but he stopped just before opening it. He had remembered there was someone else in his lodge now besides himself and Shirleen.

He crept over to where he had hung the privacy blanket and pulled a corner of it aside. Megan was asleep on her side, a blanket snuggled in her arms.

A love he had felt the instant he had first seen Megan swept through his heart again as he looked at her.

Her father had put her through a lot.

Blue Thunder vowed he would make all of that up to her.

Not wanting to keep his scout waiting any longer, especially since he was anxious to hear what Proud Horse had to report about the riverboat's arrival and departure, he stepped lightly to the entrance flap. There was no way he was going to allow that heartless demon leave the area. Earl Mingus must pay for his evil ways, and Blue Thunder was going to make certain he did!

He stepped quickly outside, to find that the sky had cleared and a half moon hung low in the sky where a short while ago lightning had flashed from cloud to cloud.

He could still smell rain in the air. Everything was dripping wet with it, which meant that the downpour had stopped only a short while ago.

"My chief, I bring news of the riverboat," Proud Horse said.

"Tell me what you found out," Blue Thunder said, placing a gentle hand on his scout's shoulder. His fringed buckskin jacket was still damp, proving that he had traveled through the rain in order to get back to his chief quickly with the news.

"The river has risen quite high," Proud Horse said. "It is impossible for the riverboat to go as close to the fort as it usually does. Word is that it will go just so far, then stop and wait for the passengers to walk to it. That will give us more time to get to the riverboat."

"That is good news for more than one reason," Blue Thunder said, smiling. "It will make it much easier to grab Earl Mingus than if we had to take him captive so close to the fort."

"But we must leave soon, because the riverboat is not far downriver from where it will stop to wait for its passengers," Proud Horse said, his eyes eager. "If you wish, my chief, I will go now and awaken the warriors who will ride with us."

"Do it quickly as I ready myself for travel," Blue Thunder said. "I want to be certain we are there waiting in the darkness of the forest when Earl Mingus takes his walk to the riverboat. While others are not watching, we will grab him and take him away."

"You will kill him?" Proud Horse asked.

"We will get far enough away from the fort, then do what we must to the man who has made my woman suffer in the worst ways possible. I have learned that he is also the one responsible for my beautiful wife's death," Blue Thunder ground out. "His death will not come soon enough for me, but first . . . he must be made to suffer before he takes his last breath of life."

He looked over his shoulder at his tepee, where his woman and her child still innocently slept, then turned back and spoke quietly to Proud Horse. "Tell my warriors that we must leave with as much silence as possible," he urged. "I do not wish to disturb my woman before we leave. I would rather she sleep as long as she can before finding me gone. The killing of this evil man must also be done in silence. Tell the warriors to arm themselves with powerful bows and arrows, but also take their rifles in case they are needed."

He kneaded his chin as he again gazed over his shoulder at the closed flap. "On second thought, I think I will awaken Shirleen," he said, slowly nodding. "But I will not tell her the true reason we are riding from the village. I would rather she not be aware of what we are doing. It would fill her heart with dread. If she does not know where we are going, she will be free to have a wonderful day with her daughter."

"What will you tell her?" Proud Horse asked, resting a hand on his sheathed knife at his right side.

"I am not one who lies easily, but today I must use a lie to keep trouble and fear from my woman," Blue Thunder replied. "I will tell her we are going on a hunt for buffalo that have been sighted nearby."

He smiled ruefully. "In a sense that will not be a lie, for we will be on a hunt, but not for buffalo. Instead we will be hunting a man with a cruel, dark heart," he said tightly. "You go. Awaken the warriors. Tell them to ready themselves. I will join you all as soon as I talk to my woman and arm myself for travel."

"It is the same as done," Proud Horse said, stepping away from Blue Thunder.

"Ask them to tell their wives the same thing I

am telling Shirleen, so that their wives will not know anything different from what my woman will be told," Blue Thunder instructed.

"They will be told," Proud Horse said, nodding.

Blue Thunder watched for a moment as Proud Horse went first to one tepee and then another.

He was proud to have such dutiful warriors, for each, after being told the plan, went back inside his tepee to arm himself and to explain their mission to his wife.

Blue Thunder went back inside his tepee. He found Shirleen just rising from their bed.

He stood there for a moment just looking at her.

Before she had gone to bed, she had taken one of her cotton gowns from the clothes that had been brought to her. It had white lace sewn onto its bodice. Her long red hair was hanging across her shoulders, and there was a look of peace in her eyes as she caught him standing there, watching her. He was over-whelmed with such an intense love for her, he was momentarily rendered speechless.

Shirleen saw the reverent way he was look-ing at her. She saw such longing in his eyes, it melted her heart. She went to him and twined her arms around his neck as she pressed her-self against him.

"I love you," she murmured. "Thank you again, my handsome chief, for all that you have done for me."

She sweetly kissed him as he brought his

muscled arms around her, his body straining hungrily against hers as he returned the kiss.

He had never felt such a strong, urgent need for a woman, but he had other things that demanded his attention today.

Making love with his woman must come later!

He gently slid away from her.

He framed her face between his hands as he gazed adoringly at her. "My woman, I was awakened by Proud Horse," he said, ready to tell the necessary lie. "He has brought news of a buffalo sighting. The rising rivers, creeks, and streams have pushed them closer to our village. Although there are many other things that are important to do, we cannot turn our backs on easy meat and hides. I am certain you understand why I must leave you so early this morning."

"Yes, I understand," she said softly. She was keenly aware of how many buffalo had been killed by white men to keep the Indians from having the pelts and meat for their families.

Shirleen had seen such a kill on her way to Wyoming, and was stunned that the slaughtered buffalo had been left upon the ground to rot. She had been horrified by the cruelty and wastefulness of the act.

"I see a future where there will be no buffalo left for the red man," Blue Thunder said thickly, as though he had read Shirleen's mind. "The white men are seeing to that by killing them off and not even taking their pelts or meat. They are purposely causing the buffalo to dwindle down to almost nothing because they do not want the red man to be able to hunt the animal. They believe that if the buffalo disappear, so will the red man."

He brushed a soft kiss across her lips, then smiled at her. "When I return, I will bring home a prime catch just for you," he said, thinking that he was not actually lying. He would be bringing a prime catch for her, but it had nothing to do with buffalo. He would not actually be bringing Earl Mingus to her, but instead the news that the man's evil had been stopped forever; that she could live a peaceful life from then on.

His smile faded. "Tomorrow, if the ground is dry enough, there will be burial rites for my uncle," he said. "We will say a final good-bye to a man who has meant so much to me and my people."

"I will be at your side as you bury him," Shirleen murmured. "That is, if you will allow me to attend a function that no white person has attended before."

"You are a part of my life now, and a part of my people's. It would be only right that you are with me as my uncle is laid to rest," Blue Thunder said. Then he moved past her and changed quickly into a buckskin shirt and leggings, sheathing a knife at his waist, positioning his quiver of arrows on his back, then taking up his bow and sliding it over his left shoulder. Then he picked up his rifle and was ready to go.

He could hear voices outside his lodge and horses' hooves, and knew that his warriors were waiting for him.

"I must go now," he said as he again brushed Shirleen's lips with kisses. "I shall return with a smile on my face over what I will catch today for you and Megan."

"I will be eagerly waiting, but not for the buffalo. For you, my love," Shirleen said, flinging herself into his arms and fiercely hugging him. "I will miss you."

"As I shall miss you," he said. He gave her another soft kiss, then turned and left the tepee.

He didn't go right to his horse, but instead to his aunt's lodge.

He stepped inside and found her busy cooking over her lodge fire. He went and knelt beside her, then told her the truth of where he was going, and why, but asked her not to tell Shirleen.

Instead, he asked Bright Sun to go and keep his woman company this day.

After his aunt agreed, he gave her a hug, then kissed his daughter and hurried outside to his saddled horse. Moments later he was riding away from the village with his warriors.

Shirleen had stepped from the tepee and watched his departure, but had also seen him go to his aunt's lodge before he left.

She had wondered why he had taken time to speak with his Aunt Bright Sun, then thought surely it was to promise her food from the hunt. Shirleen knew that his aunt was his responsibility, especially since Bright Sun now kept his daughter in her lodge, being the mother Little Bee no longer had.

Shirleen went to sit beside the fire, eager for Megan to awaken. But her child must have been extremely tired, for she still slept as deeply as she had the moment her little head had hit the comfortable pelts and blankets.

Shirleen glanced at the closed entrance flap. She realized how silent the village had become since the warriors' departure. It was as though the whole world had gone quiet until the warriors returned.

Then she heard a familiar and welcome voice. Aunt Bright Sun was outside the tepee asking for permission to enter.

Shirleen rose and hurried to the entrance flap.

She held it aside, smiling from ear to ear. She was happy not only for the food that Bright Sun had brought to her on a wooden platter, but also because Little Bee was with her. As usual she was clinging to her special doll, made exactly like the one the child had so sweetly given to her for Megan.

"Come inside," Shirleen said, stepping aside. The tantalizing smell of the food made her stomach growl.

"I have brought food and Little Bee," Bright Sun said as she set the tray beside the fire.

Shirleen smiled at Little Bee as the girl stood beside Bright Sun, staring at Shirleen.

"Has your child not awakened yet?" Bright

Sun asked, looking questioningly at the blanket that hung from the lodge poles. "Is she asleep behind the blanket?"

Suddenly a little head peeked around a corner of the blanket; then Megan rushed to her mother.

She wore a cute nightgown, with designs embroidered on it, which Shirleen had put on her while she slept.

Shirleen wove her fingers through Megan's thick, blond hair, straightening it as best she could. She would brush it later.

"Sweetie, we have company," Shirleen said, smiling. "The child's name is Little Bee and the woman is Aunt Bright Sun."

Both children were silent for a while as they stared at one another; then Little Bee saw the doll that she had brought earlier for Megan and went to it. She picked it up, walked eagerly to Megan, and put it into her arms.

"I have brought this doll for you to keep," Little Bee said sweetly. "I have one just like it. Do you want to see it?"

Megan had never been shy, and now she went to Little Bee just as the other child picked up her own doll.

"See?" Little Bee said, still smiling. "My doll and your doll are alike. They could be sisters, just like you and I could be sisters."

Shirleen was stunned by what Little Bee had said. In fact, once Shirleen married Blue Thunder, Little Bee and Megan would be sisters!

"The dolls are different from any I have ever

seen," Megan said, gazing intently at the one in her hands. "But I like it. It is cute. Thank you, Little Bee."

"Do you want to play dolls with me?" Little Bee asked eagerly. "I play dolls all the time with my friends. Will you be my friend?"

"Yes, I want to be your friend, and I would love to play dolls," Megan replied happily.

Shirleen was amazed at how quickly the two children were bonding. Their skin and hair color were very different, but to most children, such things were meaningless.

Adults would shun those of a different skin color. Even Shirleen had been guilty of that from time to time. She had always heard only bad things about Indians, but now she realized there were bad white people, just as there were bad red-skinned people, like the renegades who had come and killed her friends.

The two women and the two little girls feasted on the food that Bright Sun had brought for their breakfast. The children often giggled as they ate, filling Shirleen's heart with joy.

But then a realization vastly different from these lovely moments came to Shirleen's mind. At this very moment, Speckled Fawn was sitting vigil at her husband's side, alone, sad, and possibly afraid for her future.

Shirleen had heard Speckled Fawn worry aloud more than once about what might happen to her after her husband passed away.

"I would like to go and check on Speckled Fawn, if you wouldn't mind sitting with Megan for a while," Shirleen said. "I would like to take her some of this wonderful breakfast food, too."

"You go to her," Bright Sun urged, already on her feet and carrying the tray to the closed entrance flap. "Take this. I had planned to take her food later, but now is alright."

"Thank you," Shirleen said. She bent low and kissed Megan. "I will not be gone long. Have fun playing dolls, okay?"

Megan smiled and nodded, then seemed not even to notice when Shirleen left the tepee.

Shirleen went to Speckled Fawn's tepee and quietly spoke her name outside.

Speckled Fawn came and lifted the flap, nodding for Shirleen to come inside. She motioned toward a thick pile of pelts.

Shirleen sat down, and when Speckled Fawn sat beside her, Shirleen handed the tray of food to her.

"I am not hungry," Speckled Fawn said, ignoring the offering.

"But you must eat," Shirleen softly encouraged, feeling oddly out of place with Dancing Shadow there so close, so quiet, dressed in his finest attire for burial.

"Food is the last thing I wish to think about," Speckled Fawn said as she gazed lovingly at Dancing Shadow. "These are my final moments with my husband. I just can't eat."

"I have come to see if you are alright, and to bring you food," Shirleen said, slowly rising.

She swallowed hard as she gazed at the old, silent man.

She had seen many dead people before, lying in repose in their coffins just prior to burial. But seeing a dead body was never easy.

"Thank you," Speckled Fawn said, not rising to walk Shirleen to the entranceway. "I will remain here, keeping vigil at my husband's side until his burial."

"I understand," Shirleen said, then hurried away.

Outside, she stopped abruptly, her mind suddenly on Blue Thunder. It was known that warriors sometimes died while on the hunt. Killing buffalo could be a dangerous pursuit.

She shook such worries from her mind and hurried back to her tepee.

Her thoughts went to Earl, and she wondered briefly how Blue Thunder could have forgotten about him so quickly. Surely Earl would be leaving on the riverboat today or tomorrow, depending on how high the river had risen.

If he got away. . . . !

No, she would not think about that.

The most important thing was that Megan was finally with her, safe and sound, rescued from her brutal father!

Chapter Thirty

I'll tell you how the sun rose . . .
A ribbon at a time.

—Dickinson

Blue Thunder and his warriors had arrived just in time to see the paddlewheeler pulling in to its mooring place. They had hidden themselves and watched as several people walked across a wooden plank from the ground to the riverboat.

Blue Thunder's eyes looked carefully from person to person as each took his turn walking over the plank. The water splashed noisily against the sides of the boat, and lapped much higher than usual against the shore.

A few women screamed with fear as they inched across the plank, while others remained as long as possible on dry land, almost too afraid to move.

Blue Thunder watched the men who had also stayed behind, waiting their turn as they politely allowed the women to board first.

Thus far he had not seen Earl Mingus among

the men, yet he could see in the distance more men coming from the fort. Most of those men were uniformed soldiers, with only a few civilians among them.

These were the ones Blue Thunder kept his eyes on. Disappointment flooded his senses when he could not spot Earl among the men.

But still he and his warriors waited and watched, until suddenly a shrill whistling sound came from the boat. Everyone who had been waiting a turn was aboard, and the plank was now being hauled onto the ship.

Black smoke came from its huge smokestack, and the paddlewheels began turning, sending even more water pounding against the embankment.

The paddlewheels began turning more quickly, with water splashing from them, and the boat inched farther out toward the middle of the river. Soon it had made its way back downriver, becoming harder to see as it went farther and farther, until finally it could not be seen at all.

"The evil man did not board the riverboat," Proud Horse said as he sidled his horse closer to Blue Thunder's. He glanced at the fort, then into Blue Thunder's eyes. "What do we do now? Where should we look for him?"

"My friend, you are trusted by the soldiers stationed at the fort, so I suggest that you go and very carefully question them about this man," Blue Thunder said tightly. "Of course they will want to know why you ask, so you

can say that he had stolen a valuable horse
from your corral. They will ask you how you
knew it was he who did this, and you will tell
them you saw the man on your horse when
you were in the fort the other day. Tell them
you did not question him that day because you
had to make certain the animal was yours. Say
that you returned home and saw that the
steed was gone, and that you now hold him ac-
countable for the theft."

"That sounds like a good enough story to be
true," Proud Horse said. "These white men
look down at us, but they secretly envy our
freedom. We are not held to the same rules as
they. If they disobey, I have heard that they are
thrown in a terrible place, where rats gnaw at
their bare feet. Sometimes they are even shot.
It is not the way we do things at our village.
Rarely do any of our warriors complain about
life as we live it."

"There is one warrior who tests my patience
more than others, yet he still makes certain
that he does nothing to cause his banishment
from the tribe," Blue Thunder said, thinking of
Black Wing and the spiteful, challenging look
in his dark eyes when he openly disagreed with
his chief.

"I know which warrior you are referring to,"
Proud Horse said, frowning. "But Black Wing
has done nothing yet to cause him to be ban-
ished from our people."

"He will never go that far, for he has a wife
and children to consider," Blue Thunder said,

staring unblinkling at the fort. He reached over and placed a gentle hand on Proud Horse's shoulder. "You are dependable in all ways, my warrior, so go and see what answers you can get from the white-eyed pony soldiers about Earl Mingus."

"It is the same as done," Proud Horse said, reaching up and clasping his hand on Blue Thunder's shoulder.

Then Proud Horse wheeled his horse around and rode in the direction of the fort.

Impatient that he would have to wait for answers, Blue Thunder sighed heavily.

He dismounted, as did his warriors, then tethered his horse to a tree and walked away from the others to have a moment of privacy.

As the others dutifully waited, Blue Thunder walked farther and farther into the trees, where the thick layer of fallen, damp leaves made strange, spongy sounds beneath his moccasined feet. As he walked deeper into the forest, he suddenly got a faint whiff of smoke coming from ahead.

Curious, he walked more stealthily, his feet as quiet as a panther's paws as he moved farther into the trees. He was keenly aware that he was leaving the protection of his warriors behind him.

Yet he could not stop now that he had come this far. The smoke spiraled upward through the treetops ahead, as he could hear the faint sound of voices, and then throaty laughter.

He realized now that he was not approaching a cabin, but a campsite.

And the voices were all masculine.

He looked over his shoulder, toward where he had left his warriors and his horse, where his rifle was secured on his saddle. Although his arrows were still in his quiver, the only other weapon he had with him was a sheathed knife.

Realizing how alone he was, and knowing the danger he could be in should those at the campsite be enemies, he started to turn back, but something made him continue on a bit farther.

When he came to a clearing, he leaped back into the shadows of the trees and found himself looking at his worst enemies—the Comanche renegades and none other than Big Nose.

Blue Thunder could not believe his luck that he had happened upon the very renegades he had been hunting for so long. Though he now knew they were not the ones responsible for his wife's death, they had definitely committed countless atrocities.

Blue Thunder knew he was gazing upon a madman who was perhaps worse than any other. Big Nose and his renegade followers had surely gotten trapped on this side of the river by the higher waters. Blue Thunder was fairly certain that their hideout must be on the other side of the river, for he had never been able to find any trace of them on this side.

His heart pounding, he knew what he must do. He only hoped that he wasn't discovered before he reached his warriors. Even one wrong step onto a twig, or an alarm sounded by frightened birds scattering overhead, could spell his doom. If the renegades caught him there, alone, he would either be killed instantly or tortured terribly before dying.

Carefully, stealthily, he ran back in the direction of his warriors.

He doubted that the renegades would be going anywhere soon, for the river was treacherous now, its current much too strong to be crossed on horseback.

He would have time to return to their campsite with his warriors. He would finally avenge those people whose lives had been ended by the heartless renegades.

Breathing hard because he had run so hard and fast, Blue Thunder finally caught sight of his warriors, who were still waiting for Proud Horse's return.

He was as anxious to hear about Earl as he was to finally stop Big Nose and his renegade friends. But he could only fight one evil person at a time.

It was Big Nose who would be the first.

Wherever Earl Mingus was, he could not hide forever. Blue Thunder would never stop until he had avenged his wife's death, and the torture Shirleen had been put through at the hands of that evil, golden-haired man.

Finally reaching his warriors, Blue Thunder

stopped to catch his breath before telling them what he had seen.

One of his warriors realized that Blue Thunder needed a drink, and handed him a buckskin bag of water.

Blue Thunder nodded a thank you and eagerly took a drink.

When his thirst was quenched and he could breathe easily again, he quickly told his warriors whom he had seen.

"One of you stay behind to tell Proud Horse where we have gone. The rest of you, come with me," Blue Thunder ordered. "Secure your horses and grab your bows. Leave your rifles behind, for this must be a silent kill. I do not want the pony soldiers at the fort to know what we are doing. And we are going by foot. We will surround the renegades, and this time make absolutely certain that Big Nose does not escape as he has in the past."

The warriors all did as he told them, leaving one behind to tell Proud Horse where they were. The rest then followed Blue Thunder until they were close enough to the campsite to hear the crackling of the fire, and the loud, obnoxious voices of the renegades. One by one they took their places to surround the campsite.

Without giving any warning, they began firing arrows from their bowstrings, not giving the renegades any chance to fight back.

Soon Blue Thunder stepped out into the open and stood over the dead body of Big Nose, while his warriors went from renegade to renegade to make certain they were silenced forever.

Victorious, the warriors came together and let out loud whoops as they thrust their bows into the air over and over again.

Blue Thunder felt proud that he had finally put an end to the man he had loathed for so long. Big Nose and his companions would never terrorize the people of Wyoming again.

He gazed down at Big Nose and at the arrow that protruded from his chest. It was Blue Thunder's arrow.

He then gazed at Big Nose's open eyes, which were locked in a death stare.

"You will not kill or torture ever again," Blue Thunder said, then motioned with his head in the direction of where they had left their steeds. "Put out the fire. Leave the dead where they lie. Soon the animals and birds will have their way with them. They do not deserve a decent burial after leaving so many dead and unburied across Wyoming land."

The warriors hurried from the death scene, running until they reached their horses.

It was at that moment when Proud Horse came riding back, dismounting when he came alongside Blue Thunder.

"The man we hoped to stop today is gone, but not by riverboat," Proud Horse said as he met his chief's eyes, seeing instant disappointment in their depths. "I was told that he left the fort sometime in the night, for he was not in his cabin this morning. When the soldiers

went to invite him to eat the morning meal, he
and his daughter were gone."

Proud Horse smiled. "Also I was told that the
white woman who came to the fort was gone
too this morning," he said, chuckling. "They
believe the woman, the man, and the child
hooked up together somehow during the night
and decided to take off on their own. The pony
soldiers will not concern themselves about any
of them again."

Disgruntled, Blue Thunder hung his head.
He had so hoped to put a stop to Earl Mingus
once and for all.

Now he must search for the man.

He would not rest until Earl Mingus was
found and killed, for while he was alive, and
still living in this area, he was a constant
threat to Shirleen and her daughter Megan.

Blue Thunder looked up and turned to
Proud Horse. "You take several warriors and
search for Earl Mingus," he commanded. "But
whether or not you find the villain, you must
return by tomorrow morning, for it is then that
I will place my uncle in his final resting place."

Proud Horse placed a hand on Blue Thunder's shoulder. "If at all possible, he will be
found and brought to you, my chief," he
replied.

Suddenly Blue Thunder remembered that
Proud Horse had no idea what had transpired
in his absence. He told his most valued warrior
about the attack on Big Nose.

"He . . . is . . . dead . . . ?"   Proud   Horse

gasped, his eyes wide in wonder. The renegades are all dead?"

"Their evil deeds have been stopped forever,"
Blue Thunder confirmed. "Their bodies lie even
now as food for the forest animals and birds,
who will make fast work of their flesh. There
will be no more remaining of them than there
was of the innocent people they left behind after their killing sprees. Clothes. Bones. Even
Big Nose, with his horribly shaped and colored
nose, will no longer be recognizable."

"I heard no gunfire," Proud Horse said, lifting
an eyebrow.

"That is because there was none," Blue
Thunder replied, his eyes dancing. "Arrows are
lodged in their bodies, not bullets."

"That was clever, my chief, for gunfire would
have been heard by the soldiers at the fort,"
Proud Horse said. "Who is to say whether they
would have condoned the killing, or con-
demned us as murderers? Your plan was the
best for all concerned."

"But now, my warrior, you must leave and
search out the evil white man," Blue Thunder
said. "If you find him, silence him. But, remember, we do not want to draw undue attention to our vengeance."

Proud Horse quickly gave Blue Thunder a
bear hug, then chose the warriors who would
ride with him. With their bows slung across
their shoulders, their quivers filled with un-
used arrows, they rode away into the darkest
depths of the forest.

Blue Thunder sighed heavily. Though he was proud of what had been achieved today, he was disappointed that Earl Mingus had eluded them.

He untied his reins and held them as he swung up into his saddle. The warriors who had stayed behind did the same.

As they turned and rode back in the direction of their village, Blue Thunder was lost in thought about Earl Mingus.

What had changed Earl's mind about boarding the paddlewheeler? he wondered. Had he awakened from his drunken stupor to realize that he had been duped by a golden-haired woman, who now had his daughter in her possession?

The man had wanted to be rid of both his daughter and his wife, but he would be furious if he realized somehow that they had been reunited. He would stop at nothing to find them, and if he succeeded, Blue Thunder did not even want to think about what he might do to them.

No matter what, Earl Mingus had to be found!

He had to be killed!

Or his woman's nightmare would not be over at all.

Chapter Thirty-one

Love is a passion which kindles
Honor into noble acts.

—Dryden

January . . . Wah-nee-e-too, *winter*
Early in the Moon of Frost on the Tepee

Shirleen sat beside her lodge fire as she sewed
beads on a new pair of tiny moccasins for her
daughter. She looked up through the smoke
hole, seeing a lovely blue sky and a bright sun.
But she knew that it was quite cold outside.
Snow had fallen the entire night, and there
was now a blanket of white outside the tepee.

She had learned soon after moving to
Wyoming that winters there could be relent-
less, a time of frostbite, black ice, and dizzying
whiteouts. Bare-limbed cottonwoods stood
ghostly white near the village with snow resting on their limbs.

Shirleen smiled to herself as she thought of
the snowy wonderland the Assiniboine children had played in.

Shirleen had stood just outside the entranceway of the tepee for a while, watching

Megan teach the children of the village two games that white children played.

Megan had shown them how to make a snowman, though it lacked the usual carrot nose since no carrots were grown at this village.

A stick had been substituted for the nose, and small, round stones had been used to make the eyes and a smiling mouth.

Shirleen had smiled as her daughter taught the girls how to make snow angels. Their imprints remained in the snow, but the children were inside their warm homes now, listening to stories or playing indoor games.

Megan was at Bright Sun's tepee playing with Little Bee and would spend the night with her. The two children had become almost inseparable.

Tonight they planned to eat popped corn by the fire as Aunt Bright Sun told them the stories of her ancestors.

"Tiny Flames, what are you so deep in thought about?" Blue Thunder asked as he came into the tepee, dripping wet.

He was glad that she now used her Indian name, not the one she had been born with. It made her seem more a part of his people.

He was proud to call her not only Tiny Flames, but also his wife!

She shook her head, pale when she saw how wet he was. She had known that he planned to take a brief swim with his warrior friends, but she did not approve.

He had said it was customary for the men to

take these icy swims at least twice during the winter. They would dive into a part of the river that had not yet gotten a layer of ice over the surface.

He had explained to her that the practice kept them strong against all things.

This was the first time she had seen him dive into the river when it was so icy cold outside, and she was horrified at the prospect of his getting ill from it.

Shirleen hurried to her feet.

She grabbed a towel, which she had traded for at the fort.

"Look at you," she cried as she went to Blue Thunder and started drying him down. "How can you believe that you won't get ill from that icy swim? I wish I could talk you out of doing it, but I know I would be wasting my breath."

"It has made me feel invigorated after having to stay inside our lodge for so long a time," Blue Thunder said, his eyes dancing as Shirleen continued to fuss over him. She finished drying his body, and then set to work on his long, black hair.

"It has taken several years off my life to sit by the fire, all warm and cozy, thinking about you being in that icy water," Shirleen grumbled. "I still can't believe you did this."

"And I shall do it again when I feel my bones are getting too stiff from sitting idle by the fire during these winter months," Blue Thunder said, giving her an amused smile as she stopped and put her fists on her hips, the towel slung over her shoulder. "I think you are prettier when you are mad, for I cannot take my eyes off you, my *mitawin.*"

"That kind of talk won't get you anywhere," Shirleen said stubbornly.

"I believe it will," Blue Thunder replied, stepping out of his wet breechclout.

Now nude, his body warmed by the fire, he tossed the breechclout aside and reached for Shirleen, holding her hard against him.

The towel fluttered off her shoulder as she leaned closer to him.

"My husband, you are impossible," Shirleen said, giggling as he twined his fingers through her hair, using his grip as a way to bring her lips closer to his.

"You are my everything," Blue Thunder said huskily as his desire for her grew, the heat of his manhood pressing tightly against her. "My wife, I need you. Are our daughters at Aunt Bright Sun's lodge for the rest of the day?"

"Yes, and for the rest of the night as well," Shirleen said, breathless as he reached up inside her dress and began caressing her where she already ached for him.

She closed her eyes and sighed heavily, "My husband, oh, my husband . . ."

He quickly undressed her and tossed her clothes and moccasins aside, then picked her up and carried her to their bed of rich pelts.

He stretched her on her back beneath him as he blanketed her with his body, his eyes searching hers. His hands now moved slowly over her, causing her to draw quick breaths when he touched her more sensitive places.

"Perhaps this time we shall make a baby," he whispered into her ear, now thrusting inside her that part of him that drove her wild.

"Yes, a baby," Shirleen whispered, moving with him as his rhythmic strokes began within her. She could feel the heat of her cheeks and knew her face was flushed from the desire swelling inside her.

She tried hard not to show her disappointment each time they talked of how she had not yet become with child. They both wanted a child made from their special love for one another, and she was beginning to fear that maybe she would never be able to give him this child.

She had begun to think that the beatings Earl had given her might have somehow damaged her womb.

She hated to think he was still out there somewhere, hurting those weaker than himself. If he had taken another woman into his life, oh, how Shirleen pitied her. He was a man who seemed to take sadistic satisfaction from beating women.

When Blue Thunder had told her that Earl had disappeared without a trace, she had been horrified. She knew then that she would always have to watch closely when she was away from Blue Thunder's side, for she was certain that sooner or later Earl would reappear in her life.

She would not feel entirely free or safe again until she knew that Earl had breathed his last.

But her misgivings about Earl had not stopped her from marrying Blue Thunder. Two days after his uncle's burial they had exchanged vows. There had been three days and nights of celebrating, and then Shirleen and Blue Thunder were finally united as man and wife.

Ever since, they had shared the ultimate pleasure in lovemaking, neither of them seeming to be able to get enough of the other.

They often managed to get away alone. Megan spent a great deal of time at Aunt Bright Sun's lodge, where Little Bee still lived. To take Little Bee away from Bright Sun would have been the same as taking away her reason to live. She had grown as close to the child as though she were her very own.

Blue Thunder paused. He leaned up enough to be able to look into Shirleen's luscious green eyes. "I sense your mind is not entirely on our lovemaking," he said huskily. "Are you again worrying about our not making a child?"

"Yes, and I must confess that other things came to my mind, too," Shirleen had to admit. "I'm sorry, my husband. But I worry all the time about the fact that we have been together now for several months and I am still not with child."

"I have seen this with other husbands and wives before. They are encouraged to stop thinking about it, and when they finally are able to think of other things, suddenly, like magic, the woman does finally become with child," Blue Thunder carefully explained. "My wife, think only of how much I love you and how wonderful it is to be together. Think of the blessings we have been given, not only having found one another, but your having already given birth to such a child as Megan, and my wife having given birth to such a child as Little Bee. We are twice blessed, my wife, to have such darling daughters as our very own."

"You are so wise, so wonderful," Shirleen said, ashamed for having interrupted their lovemaking by allowing Earl into her mind again.

But when she thought about not being pregnant, who else could she blame?

"I promise that from now on I shall not think of anything while making love with you but how I am so blessed to have *you*," she murmured. "You have given my life back to me, as well as my daughter. You have made my life complete."

She reached a hand to his brow and shoved a lock of fallen hair back from his face. "My husband, if I never have another child, I promise you that I will be happy enough," she said. But even as she spoke, she knew it was a white lie. She longed for another child, and she knew that he did, too, no matter what he said.

He wrapped his arms around her and drew her more fully into the contours of his body. He kissed her passionately as he began thrusting inside her again. A husky groan came from somewhere deep inside him, proving to Shirleen that he had been able to put all they had just discussed in the farthest recesses of his mind.

She would, too, for he had ways to make her mindless. Even now, she began to writhe in response to his fiercely passionate kiss. The power of his body made her long for more.

She was breathless, her eyes closed, as she clung to him. He plunged into her, withdrew, and plunged again. He rolled one of her nipples with his tongue, and then the other, all the while not missing one thrust inside her.

She clung to his rock hardness and wrapped her legs around his waist, becoming one with him in every way. She gave herself up to the wondrous rapture as his dark, stormy eyes gazed into hers. Again he kissed her with a fierce, possessive heat.

She buried her face next to his neck, mindless as waves of bliss flooded her senses.

Blue Thunder felt the warmth of rapture rising up inside him, spreading and swelling until it blotted out all other sensations.

He clung hard to her. He placed a hand beneath her chin and lifted her face so he could kiss her precious lips again while his hard, taut body continuously moved against hers.

"I cannot hold back any longer," he whispered into her ear. "My *mitawin*, my woman . . ."

Shaken by desire, she clung to him and rode with him as her passion crested to match his. Then suddenly everything she had been feeling, the wondrousness of it, dissolved into a delicious tingling heat, spreading, searing her heart and very soul. She knew that he had found his own ultimate pleasure as his body rocked and swayed with hers, each new thrust inside her leaving them both in ecstasy.

"Again, my *mitawin*, again you have made me see that there is always something more that you give to me," Blue Thunder said huskily as he braced himself on his elbows and gazed into her eyes. "You give me the most exquisite love each time we are together."

"Then I have warmed you sufficiently after your swim in the icy river?" Shirleen asked, giggling softly as he gave her a mischievous gaze.

"I believe I need to be warmed just a bit more," he said, brushing soft kisses across her lips. "Do you have more to give?"

"I shall show you how much," Shirleen said, reaching for his manhood and cupping it within her warm hand.

She moved her hand on him, knowing that he loved for her to do this. When she did, he always got a burning look of desire in his eyes as the pleasure built within him.

He closed his eyes and let the passion fill him, then leaned up on an elbow and gave her a wicked look. He moved down her body and loved her with his tongue and mouth as he had the first time he had shown her this special way of making love.

She sighed with pleasure, closed her eyes, and slowly tossed her head from side to side as the passion built within her. Then he was over her again and his manhood was inside her.

She clung to him as he kissed her, and soon both were trembling with completion a second time as the ultimate pleasure was sought and reached.

Afterwards, they lay together beside the fire, their eyes closed. The ecstasy they had shared was unique and pure.

"I know we made a baby today," Shirleen suddenly said, causing Blue Thunder's eyes to open and look at her.

She turned on her side and giggled. "I feel it," she murmured. "I just know that what we did today made a baby."

He laughed, glad to see her so lighthearted and hopeful about the subject that usually pained her. He reached for her and held her against him. "I feel it, too," he said, hoping that what they had both felt was true.

In time they would know.

In time . . .

"My *owanyake*, handsome warrior," she whispered against his lips as she leaned closer to him. "I love you so very, very much."

"You are learning my . . . our . . . language very well," he said, laughing.

Chapter Thirty-two

She could feel as if she were
Out for the day,
As she had not done
Since she was a little girl.

—James

May . . . Moon When the Ponies Shed

Radiantly happy, so proud of the swell of her belly, Shirleen was now four months pregnant. She had left the village to pick spring flowers, loving the pretty blue lupines and wild pink roses that grew up the trunks of trees.

Every spring the aspen trees exploded with color and sound as waves of yellow-rumped warblers came north to feast on caterpillars and insects on the budding branches.

Shirleen had been amazed the first time she had looked up and seen the sheer volume of birds in the sky.

It was a feast for the eyes and ears.

Blue Thunder had seen her marvel over the birds and had told her that they came every spring to the northern forests on their way to the breeding grounds in Canada and beyond.

Shirleen laughed softly as she looked over her shoulder and saw Megan and Little Bee chasing beautiful butterflies. The girls were hardly ever apart, true sisters, as though they had been born from the same womb, created by the same mother and father.

Little Bee still slept in Bright Sun's lodge, because of their attachment to one another, while Megan most of the time slept in Shirleen and Blue Thunder's tepee.

Megan did sleep with Little Bee and Bright Sun whenever she could, for the children loved talking and laughing into the wee hours of the morning. They never seemed to lack for things to talk about.

"I have never felt as at peace as I do now," Shirleen murmured as she looked over at Speckled Fawn, whose face still wore sadness from the loss of her husband. She reached over and gently touched Speckled Fawn's arm. "One day you will be at peace again inside your heart. Each day should get easier for you."

"I know that most people see it strange that I could have loved an older man so deeply, but I did," Speckled Fawn said softly. "I doubt I shall ever love again. They say you only love once—I mean truly love—in your lifetime. Dancing Shadow was my true and lasting love."

"You are still young," Shirleen said as she slowly pulled her hand away from Speckled Fawn. "I believe you will find another man who will bring sunshine back into your heart."

"I'm not sure I would even want that," Speckled Fawn said, her eyes brightening when she saw a patch of yellow daisies a short distance away. They were growing at the edge of a thick stand of aspen trees. She walked quickly to them. "I love daisies. I want some for my lodge."

Shirleen always felt uncomfortable when she was so close to trees where anyone could be lurking.

She knew she shouldn't have wandered so far from the village, yet if she turned and looked in its direction, she could still see smoke spiraling from the smoke holes of the tepees and felt that she was safe enough.

But she would not go farther.

She must do nothing to endanger her unborn child, or her two darling girls.

"Don't go any farther, Speckled Fawn," Shirleen warned, still studying the dark shadows between the aspen trees. A soft wind suddenly blew, rustling the leaves and creating a peaceful sound that almost lulled Shirleen into forgetting that danger could be anywhere, at any time.

She was so glad that the renegades, especially Big Nose, were no longer wreaking havoc.

And no one from the fort had come to the village to question the Assiniboine about the renegades' deaths.

Sighing, standing, and waiting for Speckled Fawn to gather the last of the daisies, Shirleen marveled about the goodness of her husband. He and his Assiniboine people had accepted her and Megan completely into their lives.

And soon, ah, soon, another child would be born into their lives.

"Hurry, Speckled Fawn," Shirleen said, growing even more uneasy.

Again she gazed into the forest.

She flinched when she thought she saw movement among the shadows, and heard what might be a twig snapping.

She chided herself for being so uneasy, especially on such a beautiful spring day. She had waited a long time for such a day after having been forced to stay inside her lodge for so long due to the cold winter and early spring.

Suddenly she was aware she could no longer hear the children laughing, and her mind snapped back to attention. She grew stiff as she turned on a moccasined heel and looked for the girls.

She sighed with relief when she saw them darting in and out of tall lupines, laughing as they chased butterflies.

She hoped they knew not to wander farther than the flowers and wanted to tell them, but something warned her not to draw attention to them.

The children came into view long enough to wave at her, and then they were gone again as they ran to chase the butterflies.

Again a sound from the darkness of the aspen trees brought Shirleen around to stare into the forest. Even Speckled Fawn seemed aware of something amiss; she backed up toward Shirleen, her eyes locked on the trees.

"You heard it, too?" Shirleen whispered as Speckled Fawn stepped quickly to her side.

"Perhaps it's only a deer, or a red fox. I have seen several foxes these past days. They are so beautiful, I hate to see them killed for their pelts."

"They do seem to be so trusting," Speckled Fawn said, clutching her basket of flowers closer to her side. She laughed softly. "I think we are letting our imaginations get out of hand, thinking that what we heard was something besides a forest animal."

She turned to Shirleen. "Let's go home," she said. "I think we've had a long enough outing, don't you?"

"Yes, and enough flowers to make pretty decorations for each of our lodges," Shirleen said, laughing softly. She grew serious again. "It is so sad that you had to destroy the tepee in which you lived with your husband. It held such memories for you."

"It is the custom to take down a tepee where someone has died," Speckled Fawn said somberly. "I understand the custom, but I, too, would have loved to remain where my husband and I had sat together beside the fire."

"But I like the fact that your new lodge is much closer to mine," Shirleen said, smiling sweetly at Speckled Fawn. "We don't have so far to walk now to gossip together."

They both flinched at the same time when they heard a sound coming from behind some thick bushes nearby. What they saw next made them grab for one another as their baskets of flowers fell from their hands.

Earl stepped from behind the bushes, a

shotgun aimed directly at Shirleen's swollen belly. "Well, what do we have here . . . two of my favorite women?" he said, chuckling.

He was unaware that Megan had heard his voice and had grabbed Little Bee's hand. The two children were now running through the tall flowers behind him, toward their village.

Megan knew the danger her mother and her mother's best friend were in. She and Little Bee were going to seek help!

Earl's smile faded as he glowered at Speckled Fawn.

"Well, now, Judith," Earl said, speaking the only name by which he knew Speckled Fawn. "Ain't you the smart one? You talked me into giving up my daughter while all along planning to take her back to her real mommy." He glowered even more darkly at Shirleen, then gazed at Speckled Fawn again. "After sobering up enough to understand what had happened, I thought it over and knew that something was rotten in Denmark. I had to find out what. I just had a hunch that the woman who took Megan was connected somehow with my wife."

He heaved a sigh. "But I had no idea where Shirleen was after she was taken by the renegades. I searched around here for a while, then went to Johnson's Fort, downriver from Fort Dennison. But after thinkin' more on what happened, I began to believe that Shirleen would still be somewhere in this area, so I looked and looked. Finally I found her, as well as you, Judith, and my child."

He had been watching the girls romping and playing, and only now realized that he no longer saw them anywhere. He guessed that Megan had gone into hiding the minute she had seen her father with a gun aimed at her mommy's belly.

He would find her next, and then he'd show Shirleen that it was not the smartest thing to do to cross ol' Earl Mingus. He'd take his daughter again, but not before killing her mother and the golden-haired woman who seemed to be her best friend.

He gazed at Speckled Fawn's attire and how she wore her hair in two long braids. Then he stared at Shirleen who was also dressed like an Indian.

His eyes lingered long on her belly.

"And so you're someone's squaw, are you?" he said tightly.

He gazed past her at the smoke rising from the tepees not far away.

Then he smiled cruelly at Shirleen. "Yep, I saw you with a savage," he said. "You're living in sin with that savage, you know, because you are still legally my wife."

"I am nothing to you," Shirleen said, frowning at him. She was so afraid, she could hardly stand. "The father of my child is my husband in all respects . . . my true husband. In my eyes, and God's, you are no longer my husband. You lost the right to call me your wife after you abandoned me, and after you stole my daughter from me."

Shirleen placed her fists on her hips, trying to stare him down. "In fact, Earl Mingus, you are nothing to anybody. You are no longer a father to my Megan. The man I married is everything to me and Megan. Do you hear? Everything."

She prayed that Megan would arrive soon with Blue Thunder, for out of the corner of her eye she had seen Megan run off toward the village.

"Well, I'd never even want to touch you again after you've slept with a lice-infested savage," Earl snarled. He motioned with his rifle toward the darker depths of the aspen forest. "I have one extra horse besides my own, but both of you women can share it. I'll get you far enough away from the Injun village, and then kill you both. And to hell with Megan. I don't care what happens to her. She's been nothin' but trouble since the day she was born."

The hatred that Shirleen felt for Earl at this moment was so intense, she was ready to try to grab his shotgun, but knew she didn't have a chance against him.

And she wanted this baby that grew inside her womb so badly, she would do nothing to harm it.

She only hoped that Megan's little legs would take her to Blue Thunder in time.

"You will never get out of this alive and you are a fool if you think otherwise," Shirleen said, trying to buy time. "I'm not sure if you realize just who my husband is. He is Chief Blue

Thunder. He will hunt you down, and when he finds you, he will scalp you slowly and painfully while you are still alive, and then he will kill you."

Earl took an unsteady step away from her. He had grown pale. "I knew you were married to an Injun, but had no idea it . . . was . . . such a powerful chief," he said. "I had no idea it was his village I had been stalking. I just knew it was a village of redskin heathens and that you and Judith lived there. I even watched you from afar, and also Megan, waiting for the chance to get you."

He laughed cynically. "You probably think you've done yourself good by marrying a chief," he said.

He looked past her, at the spot where he had seen Megan hide. "Megan, come out, come out, wherever you are," he said. "If you don't, Papa is going to come for you. You don't want Papa to spank you with his belt, do you?"

Just as he spoke the last threatening words, an arrow came whizzing past Shirleen and Speckled Fawn, landing directly in the arm that held the shotgun. Earl dropped it immediately.

And then another arrow came just as quickly, sinking into Earl's stomach. He screamed in pain and fell to his knees, trying to yank the arrow from his stomach.

"You son of a bitch!" Earl cried out as Blue Thunder stepped into view, his bowstring readied with another arrow.

Shirleen hurried and grabbed up Earl's

shotgun, then stepped quickly away as Blue Thunder ran up to her side.

He held the bow steady as he glared down at the injured man. "The girls came and warned me," he said as he looked from Shirleen to Speckled Fawn, and then gazed down at Earl again. "I told them to stay with Aunt Bright Sun while I went to save her mother and Aunt Speckled Fawn."

Speckled Fawn smiled widely at her new title of aunt. Every day she felt more accepted by Blue Thunder and his people.

Shirleen gazed unblinkling down at Earl as he fell over to one side and lay in his own blood, his eyes glassy now as he looked back at her, pleadingly.

"Save me," Earl begged. "I was something to you once. Please . . . save . . . me. Your papa would want you to save me. Don't you remember? He thought I was something special."

Blue Thunder eased his bow across his shoulder and slid the arrow that had been locked on its string back into his quiver. He took Shirleen's hand. "Let us go home," he said, totally ignoring Earl as he clung to his last moments of life, begging for mercy.

Shirleen could not help staring at Earl as his breathing became slower and slower and his eyes grew dull. "What about him?" she asked, looking quickly up at Blue Thunder.

"Leave him be," Blue Thunder said coldly. "He deserves to die alone, and he will. He will die soon. He will be food for the animals that roam the darkness of night."

Earl heard that last comment. "No!" he screamed pitifully. "How . . . can . . . you be so inhumane? Shirleen, how . . . can . . . you . . . ?"

Shirleen turned away from him with Blue Thunder and Speckled Fawn at her side. Together they walked away from Earl, his screams growing weaker and weaker.

"It does seem so inhumane," Shirleen said, visibly shuddering.

"Consider who the man is, and then you will see why he should die in such a way," Blue Thunder said implacably. "I will send warriors later to make sure he is dead. When word of his death is brought to me, I shall do what is right in your eyes. I shall have him buried, but far, far away, so we will never come across his resting place. I want no reminders of him to trouble us."

Shirleen sighed with relief that Earl would get a proper burial even though she knew he deserved much less.

When they reached the outer edges of the village, Megan came running toward Shirleen.

Shirleen bent to her knees and took her daughter into her arms. "The nightmare is now truly over," she murmured into Megan's ear. "My *micinski*, you can sleep well at night now, and you can run and play free of worry that your father may suddenly appear to abduct you.

My darling daughter, we have both been freed of a demon."

As Blue Thunder stood there smiling, he watched mother and daughter embracing lovingly.

He was glad he had been able to stop Earl Mingus in time today, or all would have been lost, not only for Shirleen and Speckled Fawn, but also for himself.

He would not be able to live through the death of another wife!

Epilogue

We'll live our whole young life away
In the joys of a living love.

—Wilcox

Several Years Later

Blue Thunder's Wind Band of Assiniboine had been forced to move from their homeland as more land was grabbed up by the white government.

Blue Thunder had vowed never to put his mark on any papers that were offered to him by whites. He had learned that most treaties weren't honored.

He had chosen to take his people high into the mountains of Montana, where no whites dared to venture, although winters were worse there.

At the Assiniboine village, located near a beautiful waterfall that splashed far down into a river, there were enough warriors to provide their people with food, firewood, and clothes. Chief Gray Eyes had brought his people, with their powerful warriors, to join forces with

Blue Thunder's people for the protection of both tribes.

Gray Eyes and Blue Thunder shared the duties of chieftain and felt doubly powerful against the white-eyed pony soldiers.

Although Speckled Fawn was somewhat older than Gray Eyes, he had taken her as his *mitawin*, his wife. They were content, but childless. Speckled Fawn could bear no children but they shared Blue Thunder's and Shirleen's children, which now numbered six.

One more daughter had been born to them, then three sons.

The daughter's name was Sweet Wind, their sons' names were Night Moon, Swift Fox, and White Wolf.

Megan had become quite a tomboy, who challenged her brothers in every way possible, while Little Bee was delicate and very ladylike.

Blue Thunder and his people's happiness had been lessened when Aunt Bright Sun had suddenly died two winters ago; her heart had just given out.

Little Bee now lived in the same tepee as her parents, brothers, and sisters. Happiness overflowed within the lodge of the great chief Blue Thunder and his wife Shirleen, who was now called Tiny Flames by all who knew her!

WIN A WONDERFUL GIFT!

To celebrate the publication of my 100th book, *Savage Skies*, I am giving you, my readers, a chance to win a beautiful Indian turquoise choker and earring set. My heroine in *Savage Skies* is wearing the choker on the inside cover painting of *Savage Skies*.

If you wish to put your name into a drawing for a chance to own this beautiful choker and earring set, send your proof of purchase (receipt) for *Savage Skies*, and a postcard with your name, address, and phone number, as well as the page number on which the necklace is mentioned in *Savage Skies* to:

Cassie Edwards
6709 North Country Club Road
Mattoon, IL 61938

The deadline for this drawing is December 3, 2007. I, personally, will notify the winner by phone. Good luck to you all!

Always,

Cassie Edwards